DEMON N MY HEAD

GERALD BROWNING

I0543705

NIGHT TO DAWN

Night to Dawn Magazine & Books LLC
P. O. Box 643
Abington, PA 19001
www.bloodredshadow.com

Print ISBN: 978-1-937769-05-5
Digital ISBN: 978-1-937769-01-7

Copyright 2011 by Gerald Browning

Cover art: Teresa Jay
Editor: Barbara Custer
Printed in the United States of America
Worldwide Electronic & Digital Rights
1st North American, Australian and UK Print
Rights

Gabriel Brimstone stalked the pages of Night to Dawn for years. This book is dedicated to those who have helped me along this journey. Mom, you taught me how to read and write. This is for you. Dad, you taught me character, without which, Gabriel would not have been born. Thank you for that. Monica, you have taught me compassion and I will never forget that. Also, there have been many who have helped me along, who have listened to the characters in this book as they have evolved. The Flint Area Writers, thank you for encouraging me to write and to tell me when I have been wrong.

Many people have believed in me, even when I did not believe in myself. Those at Knollwood, you have helped me in ways I cannot imagine. This is for you. Jennifer, and the Edwards family (Barbara and Vernon), you took me into your home and treated me with love and compassion and for that I give you the same. Your drive bore this book in more ways than I can articulate. Thank you for believing that I could succeed. Jennifer, you have listened to my thoughts, dreams and deepest hopes. You have made me happier than I have ever been. This is for you.

Those that still live on the streets of Chicago; we have shared dreams and nightmares. Of which, Culver's Bay was born. You are eternally in my heart. And last, but not least, Barbara Custer, you saw my dream and helped to turn it into a reality.

Finally, this book is for Margo Lagattuta, who taught me how to write with heart. Keep putting the heart before the course.

Prologue

You read these words passively and as such, you feel as if you will be transported into a world unlike that which you have ever seen or heard. You think that you will be privy to a story that will take you from your troubles, but you couldn't be more wrong. This story is an active one. Once you have opened this book you have become an active participant. As you shall see, knowledge is a dangerous thing and it demands action.

Know thyself. The Oracle of Delphi warned Oedipus of this and he did not heed this warning. This is a warning/word of advice, depending on which side of the book you feel that you are on. This bit of advice was not taken by a man named Gabriel Brimstone, a man who struggles with an inner demon that we all have to struggle with at some point in our lives ... addiction.

What is an addiction? What is your addiction? To the afflicted, is it a monster? Is it an imp that sits on your shoulder, constantly tempting you to succumb to your deepest desires? Who among us does not have that imp, that voice, that Id whispering to us to commit acts of immorality?

Be it alcohol, drugs, sex, or something ... else ... we have that guilty pleasure. Some of them are less harmful: a reality show, shopping, etc. Others are, if left unchecked, horrifying and can create monsters. The alcoholic, the pedophile, or even ... the killer.

Do these addictions make us who we are?

1

Or do we make them?

Gabriel Brimstone was tracking a different kind of monster in Culver's Bay. A kind of monster that is an addiction. A kind that you know but deny its existence.

A vampire.

By the time you put this book down, after reading its blood-soaked passages, you will come to realize that vampires, demons, and haunted souls are all too real. They are as tangible as the text that you are holding in front of you. Just as real as I am.

I grin as I pen these words in blood, cutting open the flesh along Gabriel Brimstone's body and dipping my pen into his life fluids and scrawling my words across the canvas of skin that is this journal, his journal. You will read this and convince yourself that this is the work of a lunatic. Just like vampires, you will think Gabriel as fictional or mad. However, I can tell you that the ruminations of the mad, demented, or whatever term you choose to label them, have more of a connection with reality than what you may think.

By reading these words and learning what you are about to learn, you will realize that your reality is just a lens. That lens has edges; there are boundaries to your reality – to your sanity. This tome will stretch those boundaries. I invite you to turn the page and plunge into the reality of the man that you will come to know as Gabriel Brimstone...

Learn of his addictions ... his passions ... his life ... and his ruin.

Step One

"We admitted we were powerless over alcohol – that our lives had become unmanageable."

The smell of cigarette smoke mingled with desperation, creating an aura of shame that was overwhelming and inspirational. Each story of the fellow members moved me, making me realize just how similar to others I was. It made me feel human.

I've never felt this way.

A tall, slender man with sunken cheeks, hollow eyes, and yellowish skin finished his story of how the bottle claimed him. The liquid hypnotized him before he took a drink.

His name was Mike L.

He was an alcoholic.

Now, he's dead.

Mike spoke about his wife, Leanne, and their two children. Leanne packed up the kids and left for her mother's house after his last drunken stupor. He'd been sober for three weeks.

"Every day is a battle." Mike stared through tear-filled eyes.

Amen, I thought.

You are pathetic! the Voices taunted.

Not now, I thought. *Not here!*

You think you are a pathetic human drunk? What a laugh. You are more than these pitiful creatures. You could slaughter these beasts within moments. Slake your thirst! Give in to the primal passions. Imagine a chorus of whispers in your ear. For seven years, I've had to endure this. I wage a war inside my head every day.

Much like the war I wage outside in the "real" world.

My name is Gabriel Brimstone.

I am a living vampire.

****

"My name is Rachel, and I'm an alcoholic."

The young woman wore a tight t-shirt, black jeans that covered even her shoes, a long black trench coat, and enough chains to weigh her down about ten pounds, not to mention the metal that stabbed through her face.

Her emerald eyes glowed. They were spaced apart, yet large enough to give her a doe-like innocence. Her small nose and rounded cheeks made her look young, but the slight lines on her hands put her at about thirty. She was five feet seven inches with a curvy figure.

Succulent, the Voices reminded me.

Rachel began her story of a high school student lured into the wrong crowd, the wrong parties, and the wrong guys. She began to experiment with drugs and alcohol. Before she knew it, she dropped out of college, was kicked out of her mother's house, and forced to survive by running drugs.

No one will miss her. Their seductive voices tempted me with visions of her grappling limbs fighting for life mixed with whimpering cries as I drained her of life. Saliva filled my mouth as I locked onto her. I had forgotten to listen to what she was saying. I barely noticed Mike leave the room that was rented in the basement of the YMCA. The room was spartanly decorated. A lectern for the speakers and the MC, an ex-football player named Hayes Sanders, sat between a chalkboard and the audience. To our right stood a flimsy folding table with a coffee maker, Styrofoam cups, and a box once filled with sandwiches. I could only focus on her plump, red lips, hair that fell in waves to the tip of her shoulders, and voluptuous figure. When the group stopped clapping and she smiled after her mouth finished moving, I realized her speech was over. I clapped self-consciously, acutely aware that she sat in front of me.

I didn't notice Mike leave.

I tapped Rachel on the shoulder, put on a smile that I hoped was disarming, but felt sheepish. "Th-thank you for sharing."

She blushed. "Thanks." She turned in her chair and crossed her denim clad legs. Her exposed skin was pale. The Goth look enhanced her beauty. "I'm Rachel," she said, extending her hand.

"Gabe." Our hands met. *Feel the blood coursing through her.* "It's n-nice to meet you."

"You too."

The piercing scream caused me to spring up a flight of stairs to the exit door of the building. I almost grabbed the Beretta from the waistband of my jeans, but the other members of the AA group with me stopped me. When we reached the back door that led to an alley, Mike's body cooled on the concrete.

"Jesus!" an alcoholic named Ted yelled as we gathered around the body. Hayes was on his cell phone, placing a 911 call.

A wave of energy crashed around us that only I could feel. Rachel rubbed her hands over her arms. Hayes took his sports jacket off and draped it across her shoulders. When he finished the call, we gathered up the nerve to move closer. When a member turned Mike's head to the side to display two puncture wounds in his neck, my fears were confirmed.

"A vampire?" Ted wondered.

"Not a real vampire." This came from Jack, a balding man with a pear-shaped body and a thick mustache. He stared at Ted. "There's no such thing. It's a psychopath. He's obviously delusional and uses the vampire mythos to act out his fantasies."

Did I mention Jack was a therapist?

We know the truth, don't we, Gabriel? We do exist, and they fear us. My heart thudded in my chest. The demons that prey upon humankind lived in The Nightside, a world that existed only when the sun went down. They hide in the shadows, using the light of the moon and stars to stalk.

I tracked a demon couple to Culver's Bay with the intentions of finishing what was started over a year ago. Being powerless to save Mike's life made my resolve to finish this much grimmer.

The distant sirens of prowlers made me want to vanish. I had no social security number and my phony driver's license wouldn't pass a close scrutiny. I waited until every pair of eyes in the group was focused on Mike's body, and then disappeared. My mission in Culver's Bay was unfolding. I felt as if I was being led like the proverbial horse to water. Was I going to drink?

Things were adding up too conveniently for me. I *know* I was supposed to be here. I *know* Mike's body was a message for me.

It was a message sent by the Baltimores.

****

Nathaniel and Miranda Baltimore were newlyweds who happened to be stranded by the side of a road in a sleepy, little town called Tallmadge. They barely survived an attack by Valimus, a vampire I'd been hunting. Miranda was bitten and losing blood. I tracked the attack to a local library. When we returned to their motel room, Valimus trapped me and allow Miranda, who was seduced by the Virus, to turn her husband.

It was that night when I found out what I was.

I thought of this as I stood on the rooftop of the Falcon Building, a seven-story steel, glass, and iron office building. I watched the coroner's van pull into the Culver's Bay Police Department's parking lot. The van carried Mike's corpse. The virus had an incubation period of forty-eight hours. Since Mike was a frail man, it would take longer to reanimate him.

Mike would be in the ground when he woke up.

I have seen corpses claw their way out of a grave. It's not as easy as the movies suggest. The casket, especially if the family cares about the dead, is difficult to escape. Some demons have broken their fingers trying to get out. Let's say you *don't* go mad with claustrophobia. Let's suppose you break through the casket. You've got six feet of caked earth ahead of you. Just the thought of so much malleable earth spilling through the nostrils, mouth, and ears is enough to send chills down my spine.

****

"Just one more."

"I can stop whenever I feel like it."

The confessors said the same thing again and again at the meetings. Addiction: it's an all-consuming disease. It is a cancer.

Every day is a battle.

The motel I stayed at wasn't a flophouse, but it was close. Mike's obituary was printed in papers two days after his body went to the morgue. The funeral was earlier that afternoon. The scream jolted me from my sleep. I hadn't realized I dozed off, but the echoes of her scream pulled me back into a reality that wasn't my own. Was it sleep, or another of my blackouts? I'd been having them a lot more lately than usual and it started to alarm me. Was it the Council? Was it another of their tricks? Was it Valimus? Did he have powers that had yet to be revealed? A power pulsed within this city, a supernatural power. It called me here.

My cleaned Beretta 9mm lay on the rickety bed, atop an oily rag, alongside seven magazines filled with 9mm hollow pointed silver bullets. Silver throwing daggers beside them. All of them were made in the shape of crosses. They were gifts from a gunsmith I knew in Los Angeles. I told him that crosses and other holy paraphernalia could not harm the fiends.

"You can never be too careful," he replied.

Only a few things can kill a vampire. Sunlight works like a charm. The ultraviolet radiation reacts to the Virus within their system, causing it to become unstable and burn from the inside out. I've killed many bloodsuckers this way and let me tell you, it's a gruesome way to die. Much like the movies, they become kindling.

As the weapons suggest, the fiends of the Nightside (i.e. werewolves, vampires, demons, etc.) are allergic to silver. The lore says that silver is the metal of God and that is why it can kill all things impure. For some reason the Nosferatu Virus is killed by silver (or silver nitrate). Coating the bullets in silver does a world of good when dealing with them.

However, the stronger the vampire is, the more silver I need to kill them. I've only killed a handful of Masters (vampires that have been around for more than a hundred years). The longer they exist, the more blood they consume; therefore, the more power they have.

They are *evolving*.

Will they evolve to the point where silver will do nothing to them?

The final way to kill a vampire is decapitation. The old adage is true: cut off the head, and the body dies. At the Facility, I have seen "experiments" beg for mercy as the doctors removed their hearts. None of them survived having their heads removed. Their tests gave me the insight to effectively destroy them.

Well, that and the strain of the Nosferatu Virus that has blended in with my genetic code. It altered my DNA, making me neither human nor undead.

Wesley Snipes makes it look so easy in those crappy movies.

I watched, from my motel room window, as the sun sank from sight and darkness swallowed daylight. As the darkness draped the cityscape, my bone-weary fatigue left me. An unnatural energy filled me like water in a glass. One of the problems of The Nosferatu Virus was that I was very tired when the sun was out. I gained superhuman strength and vitality after sunset.

I would need all the strength I could get.

Walking over to the bed, I looked at the newspaper that lay next to the Beretta. *"Tooth Fairy Strikes Again!!!"* Another monster was on the prowl, but this one was a lot closer than I'd like to admit. The press was almost as formidable a foe as the vamps. I stared at the sack of teeth that laid in the duffel bag that became my closet, armory, and home.

****

At 9:45 p.m., I reached Meadowrest Cemetery. I stopped the Cavalier I was driving at the gates and walked across the threshold. Once I entered the resting place, a current of energy raised the hairs on my arms. I had the odd feeling that a compass feels when its arrow is drawn to magnetic north. I took a deep breath, closed my eyes, and followed the power.

The energy slammed shut. I opened my eyes and was standing seven feet away from Mike's recently filled grave. Rachel's appearance was more staggering than the sudden energy recession. She stood before the grave wearing a long, black, leather trench coat. The collar was turned up against the chill. She spun around to face me. Her shocked face spilled with relief and recognition.

"Gabe, I-I wasn't expecting you." She glanced at Mike's tombstone. "But I'm glad you came."

"I have to be here."

Rachel nodded. "It was a beautiful ceremony, you know. Leanne, Richie, and Sam were there. Leanne even apologized to us for leaving him."

"Why?"

"She was having an affair. They're not … weren't … officially divorced."

"She brought her lover with her to the funeral?"

"No." She was a statue. Her raven hair was living tendrils, whipping across her lovely features.

"Then … how?" My voice was gentle.

"I could tell by her eyes. They looked so guilty. She knew she did Mike wrong." I did not know what else to say, so I kept my mouth shut.

"Fair enough," was all I said. I did not know his wife, nor did I care how she felt about her husband. All I wanted to do was focus on the mission.

"What brought you here?"

"I wanted to pay my respects."

I felt Michael waking up.

"Th-there was just … nothing." She hugged herself. I waited for the Voices to taunt me, to tell me to drink her dry. My mind was at peace.

Rachel shook her head and laughed. "I've been reading too many vampire novels."

"Listen, Rachel, if you think there's such a thing as vampires and … faeries—" I tried to sound convincing, but she cut me off before I could continue.

"I don't even want to get into that. I mean … just *looking* at a dead body …" She trembled. "They make … death … sound so … romantic."

"Death and sleep are two different things, no matter what Shakespearean tragedies tell you. Mike paid a price to find his peace." A chill blew through the cemetery followed by a wave of power wafting from the dirt before Mike's tombstone. "It's chilly. You need to go."

"I-I guess so." She pulled her coat closer. I mentally screamed at her to hurry up. When I stopped at the threshold, she asked, "Aren't you leaving too?"

I shook my head, putting on a smile. "I've got to say goodbye."

She nodded again. After an awkward silence she said, "I would like to see you again, Gabe."

"I'm at the Roadside Motel. Give me a call. Room Six." I walked away.

"Gabe?"

"Yeah."

"Do you believe in Heaven?"

"Not for me." I headed for Mike's grave, with my cold hand underneath the jacket, gripping Death.

****

Fingers wriggled through the packed earth like thick worms. I kept the Beretta in my right hand and grabbed the wrist that appeared. I pulled Mike out of his grave. He shivered and retched into the soil. The demon moaned and screamed as he felt rigor mortis crack his joints.

"Dear God!" His voice box was ruptured.

"God has nothing to do with this."

The alcoholic shivered. "Gabe? Is that you? What are you doing here? What am I doing here? What's going on?" It made sense that the newly undead would be inquisitive.

I did not want to play Twenty Questions with it. All I wanted to do was kill the damned thing.

Mike's eyes darted. Except for being covered in dirt and wearing a cheap suit with a long slit up the back, he looked relatively normal.

"You were attacked. What do you remember?"

"Wha …?" Mike tried to focus, but his senses were overloaded. What was once background noise was now an explosion. The fabric of his suit was scraping against his sensitive skin. The night was lighter and less intimidating, almost … comforting.

"Mike!"

"Not so loud, Gabe. I feel like shit. Did I … have a relapse?" He looked around on the ground, trying to find a liquor bottle. "I let everybody down. Oh, Lord, how did I let it beat me? I mean, I'm still depressed about Leanne and all—"

I did not have the patience to continue to listen to his prattle, but I could not just shoot him without giving a reason.

"You did not drink, Mike. This is about another one."

"Another … addiction?"

"Yes." None of this was his fault. "What do you remember?"

"Th-there were two of them. A man and a woman. Both well dressed. Nobody dressed like that should be down here in The Ways." The YMCA was located in an area called "The Ways." All of the streets ended with "way," like Broadway, Causeway, etc.

I asked him to describe the couple. His description matched the Baltimores.

They must've known I was attending the AA meetings and wanted to send me a message.

It was my decision to follow The Baltimores to Culver's Bay. It was my decision to attend the meetings. It was my decision to interact with the people. It was my fault that Mike was a target.

Now, he's dead. The problem was his body did not know it.

"Do you know them?"

"I've been tracking them for a while." I might as well give him the truth. What harm would it do? He's already dead.

The Beretta weighed heavy in my waistband, reminding me of my job.

"Tracking? What're you, a bounty hunter or somethin'?"

"Or something," I answered.

Mike's eyes locked onto his tombstone. He stared at it incredulously. His slack jaw moved, but nothing came out. "Whwhat's going on?"

"Those two people you ran into? Do you remember them attacking you?"

Mike thought for a moment. "N-no. Nothin'."

That wasn't uncommon in a vamp attack. The confused look on his face told me he was getting too much information for his mind to process so quickly. "What's going on? Why is that ... tombstone there?"

"Those two people killed you, Mike. You are ... dead."

"What?" He shook his head. "I can't be dead. I'm walking around. Talking." He got to his feet. His legs buckled and he fell to his knees. He looked at his tombstone and the hole from where he climbed. "But … how?"

"You are infected."

"How?" He paused as the realization dawned on him. "That couple," he whispered. "The woman…"

"What did she do?" I knew the answer, but he needed to discover it himself.

"She … she …" His hand rose to the right side of his neck. "Am I a … a … vampire?" The last word was a whisper.

"Yes," I said sadly.

"What … happens to me?"

Mike stared at my weapon. He looked up at me in fear, and raised his hands, like in the movies. He did not know me or my reputation since he thought he had a chance on living.

"L-look, Gabe. I haven't killed anybody."

"Yet."

"I won't … I won't drink anybody's blood."

"How do you know? You were an alcoholic. The booze will not work on you anymore. You won't get a buzz. You will never feel warm. You will not forget who you are. None of the things you sought by drinking will be gained by the bottle."

"Why?"

"Your body is different now."

"But—"

"You will learn to crave it. Blood will be your addiction." My voice held so much weight. I could feel my own pain in the words I spoke. Mike stared at me through yellowing eyes. His pale skin, sharp cheekbones, and tight thin lips made him look like the walking corpse that he was.

"No, I won't. I promise."

I stepped closer to him, and we locked eyes. The sudden brightening of the night told me my eyes had changed color. Mike reeked of fear. "You will submit to the Addiction.

We all do."

"Y-you're one of them."

"Not quite."

"Please don't kill me." Tears formed in the corners of his eyes.

"You are a slave to the Addiction. You will *need* the blood. It will become your reason for being." Almost a year ago, I fell into a trap devised by Valimus and The Baltimores. I was trapped with a wounded woman and I drained her. I do not remember killing her.

However, I recall killing her again that morning.

The coppery taste of blood stayed in my mouth long afterwards. It rolled around my tongue and filled my mouth. Mike was sincere about his vow, but he would not follow through with it. Addicts are vulnerable. Whether it is alcohol, drugs, sex, or blood; we will get it when we're desperate.

He wasn't desperate yet.

"Y-y-you can't do this. I've got a family."

"You would kill them all."

Fear mingled with rage. "I would *never* do that!" He rushed me, but because of his weakened state, I was able to side-step him.

"You know about addiction and cravings, but you do not know about this! This is tied into your ... life! You must kill to live."

"I can go to a blood bank."

"That won't last," I told him. "You'll see a rat or a cat and kill it. Pretty soon you'll want that. Do you know why?"

"Why?"

"You'll feel its heartbeat slowing. You will realize that you are, in fact, stealing its *soul*. You'll *crave* it." I did not realize I was walking towards him and pointing the gun at his chest. "You will get off on the hunt. It won't be about the kill anymore. It'll about the hunt. That's when you will realize you are a predator." Mike began to protest, but I continued. "Months will go by, but one night you will wake up and want more. You will go for bigger prey. No one will miss a bum here or a crack addict there. No one will think twice about a rapist or a molester. One day, you will look at yourself in the mirror as you're washing your hands and it will hit you that no matter how many times you wash them, the blood will never come off."

"That's not me. You don't know that. That is your addiction, but I would never take an innocent life. Gabe, my … my lips are so parched. May I have something to drink?"

I shot him in the forehead with a 9mm silver bullet. The back of his head splattered against his tombstone as he fell towards his grave.

I approached his cold body and pocketed the weapon. From my other pocket, I withdrew a pair of rusty pliers. I took his fangs in silence, placing them in a leather satchel that I kept on me at all times.

To the darkness, and my newest victim, I admitted the first thing I learned from the meetings. It is our first step: "We admitted we are powerless over alcohol – that our lives had become unmanageable."

Well, alcohol … and other fluids.

Once my grizzly work was done, I allowed the shadows and fog to envelope me. I was left alone with the dead. Moving through the utter stillness, I heard her screams yet again. Try as I might, I could not push them away.

Step Two

"Came to believe that a Power greater than ourselves could restore us to sanity."

"I've been out of town for a while and I was working with a therapist before I left. When I got back, I found out he was gone. Since ... *we* ... run in the same pack, I was hoping you could help me find him." Dr. Jack Worth's office was decorated in masculine colors, dark oaks, black, and a marble desk. He wrapped his degrees and knowledge around him like a protective blanket. It was so easy to see through his façade, to the insecure little man with something so dangerous to hide.

"Oh." He looked relieved, but he shouldn't have been. His condescending smile reappeared. "Sure, Gabe. Did he work here?"

"Yeah. His name is Dr. David Winthrop."

"Really?" He grew nervous. The doctor knew him. "Dr. David Winthrop" was a pseudonym for a bloodthirsty vamp that I had taken care of months ago.

I still hear his screams.

"What's wrong?"

"Nothing. I'll get on it. I know we have some files in archives that the staff keeps. I'll go through them. Is there a number I can reach you at?" He stared at the large spike shaped as a cross that hung round my neck. It matched several of them that I hid upon my person. It wasn't *just* for style. They were highly effective for killing vampires.

"No. I'll look for it at the next meeting." I stood up and shook his hand.

"Are you sure? I mean if you give me your address- "

I shook my head again. "I don't want to impose. I'll just get it from you … at the *meeting*." It was the same night I was scheduled to meet The Baltimores, a pair of vampires I had been tracking for months now. There were times when I felt an invisible hand guiding me in a particular direction. Maybe it was The Council, a group of vampires in charge of the undead population. I would not put it past them to do this. At least I felt like my hunt was going somewhere. If Jack was going to do what I asked, I may get some valuable information. The paranoid part of me saw how nervous Jack was. Why was he so adamant about getting my address?

On the way out, I observed people talking about Amhearst Institute. In the waiting area, a few brochures sat on tables. *Interesting*, I thought.

You catch on quickly, Mr. Brimstone. Multiple laughers echoed in my skull. They knew my thoughts and my very actions. Part of me knew I was doing exactly what they wanted me to do. I was doing what I was bred to do. *How do you fight something that is bigger than you? How do you wound something that controls your actions? Can that "something" restore you to who you were … or who you are supposed to be?*

****

I prowled the streets of Culver's Bay in my stolen Cavalier; I recalled the wallet I had also stolen from Dr. Winthrop, who happened to be a vampire named Malfric. The wallet contained several hundred dollars and a few credit cards, which I never used since they are easy to trace. Large wad of bills were winnings from his high rolling venture. After a year of using his funds to bankroll my quest, I had nearly five hundred dollars left.

In a hidden pocket of the wallet, was a photograph of a beautiful woman with long, red hair. Her eyes were the color of freshly cut grass. Her skin was tanned and glowed. Her face held a crafty intelligence. This woman was Jessica Winthrop, the wife of the fiend. There was one huge coincidence that spoke volumes to me: Winthrop's address was in Culver's Bay.

I drove to 1592 Oakwood Drive. The sun had set about two hours ago, and I sat in my car and stared across the street. The lights in the downstairs living room and kitchen lit up the house.

You're just wasting your time. Multiple voices were whispering in unison, like an unholy choir. I looked at the Beretta in the passenger seat. The butt protruded from a copy of the Gazette. I wasn't sure what I was doing here. The psychic trail went cold.

Why don't you find that nice Rachel girl and drain her body?
Sadists! When I get my hands on you-
You will do nothing because you cannot do anything. We are many. You are only one inept detective.

I was smart enough to realize that the Voices wanted me out of the neighborhood for a reason. That reason showed up nearly five minutes later when a black BMW pulled into the driveway. My heart fluttered as Jack Worth exited the car.

The therapist waddled to the doorstep and rang the bell. The door opened and the picture of the woman in Winthrop's wallet allowed Worth inside. Even from the dim light of the porch, I could see her hair sparkle. I stopped gripping the wheel as it threatened to snap under my strength. The urge to grab my weapon was overpowering. I wasn't even sure what was going on and I was ready to "resolve" the problem with bloodshed. What did that say about me?

What did that say about the Power that compelled me to be here?

I grabbed the gun and jumped out of the Cavalier. In most cars, a little overhead light would come on once the door was opened. However, I pressed the button on the rearview mirror that deactivated the light, plunging the car into soothing darkness.

I jogged across the street with the 9mm in a firm grip. Every fiber of my being told me to break the door down and blow Dr. Worth to hell, but I knew that was the irrational side of me. I crouched lower as I reached the porch. The curtains in the windowsill were parted, allowing me to see the profiles of Worth and the redhead. They sat on the couch right in front of the window.

"How are you doing?" He sounded mundane.

"I'm fine, Jack." She returned his blandness.

"It's been awhile since we last talked."

The woman snapped. "Don't you take that tone with me."

"What tone?"

"David had that tone in his voice every time we got in an argument. That holier-than-thou, psycho-babble, condescending tone. When you said you wanted to come over and talk, I thought you wanted to do it as a friend, not as a damned shrink." Her movements were erratic. I saw the fire seeping into her eyes.

"I'm sorry. I guess I have a hard time keeping the work in the office." After an awkward silence, Jack said, "Can you forgive me?"

The anger slid off her face like syrup. A petite smile curled her lips. "It's okay. I-I just hate not knowing." She played with her wedding ring. "I mean, he's been gone for almost a year. He just told me he would be at a convention in Las Vegas and-and…" Jack Worth rushed to her side and wrapped his arms around her. She shivered and clutched onto him like a life preserver.

At that moment, a young boy with sandy blond hair ran down the staircase next to the living room. He ran to the redhead and asked, "Mommy, where's Daddy?"

Daddy?

Impossible! my mind cried. *They can't procreate. You can't do this!* I cried to God.

It was no wonder The Council hid this from me. That means they had a different method of evolving. I could hear my blood pumping through my body at an alarming rate. Every ounce of me was focused on the tableau unfolding before me.

I did not notice the vampire that grabbed me by the collar of my jacket and yanked with all of its might. The force flung me twenty feet across the front lawn and into the street. Once I crashed against the hard pavement, the wind rushed from my lungs.

I should have smelled it before it could touch me, let alone fling me across the Winthrop front lawn. I cursed myself as I tried to force the air back into my lungs. Like a turtle, I tried to roll onto my side, but the demon kept me from doing so with a foot on my chest. The fiend leaned forward. The shift in weight felt as if someone placed a brick wall atop me. If it applied any more pressure, I would crack a rib.

The vampire smiled, openly displaying his incisor fangs. He wore a pair of blue jeans, a black sweater and nice sneakers. His hair was black and fell in long curls down his back. His skin was paper white. The demon's eyes were rubies glimmering in the darkness. "Tell me this is not *the* Gabriel Brimstone that has killed nearly three hundred of the Kissed. You cannot be the same one that has entire broods whispering his name before the sun rises." The monster slammed its foot against my chest. If I did not have the Virus, my chest would have caved in.

The demon bent forward and smacked me across the face. The blow left me lightheaded. My vision blurred and for a brief instant the demon's face was stretched taut, as if it was a piece of leather. The jaw grew longer and its fangs protruded from its face. After multiple blinks, the face returned to its normal state.

"No wonder Valimus has been able to run circles around you." The monster laughed at me. Instinct told my body to reach for the Beretta at my waistband, but it was gone. The vampire's glowing red eyes darted to my right. I followed his line of sight to the handgun. "You are impotent without your gun."

A moment after that, the blade was planted in the center of the foot that rested atop my chest. He howled to the night sky as I rolled away from the bloodsucker. My gun, which had skidded into the street, was now within reaching distance. I grabbed it, took aim, and fired off a single shot.

The demon was already in motion. Instead of pulling the knife out of his foot, he merely ran with it stuck in the center of his shoe.

The monster was a blur, but I knew I hit him in the shoulder. It disappeared into the night.

****

I had to start my investigation somewhere. What better place than back at The Milton Center for Mental Health? Jack was involved in this so deep he would never see daylight. As soon as I got cleaned up and dressed, I took a cab over to The Milton Center and got out looking up at the sun, I realized that I did not feel tired.

Why? I wondered. Was this the grace of God that bestowed the Power onto me, allowing me to continue with my mission?

Or was it something else?

Focus on the task at hand, I told myself. I entered the ramp structure and took a nearby stairwell to the underground floor. I could keep an eye on the building and stay in the darkness.

The lower floor was dark and murky. A handful of overhead light fixtures barely lit the structure. The concrete walls kept the area cool.

The hairs on the back of my neck stood on end. A coolness wrapped around my body like a cold silk sheet. A million needles of preternatural energy stabbed into me.

A vampire was nearby.

"Their teeth!" The disembodied voice filled the lot.

I ached to use the Beretta, but in broad daylight in the city, the police response would be quick. I wanted to interrogate him. Without making a sound, I slipped two cross-shaped knives into my hands. They were the perfect balance for throwing and were made from pure silver. A friend of mine made them for me in Los Angeles and I was anxious to try them out.

"My foot still hurts. It burns every single time I put weight on it. But it's not as bad as the bullet wound." His voice was full of hate.

"I rarely get feedback from my victims. I appreciate the comment."

"It doesn't hurt as badly as what you did to them. You took their teeth!" There were so many of them. There were times when I did take their teeth. Vampires, as many times as you shoot, stab, or burn them, keep coming back. But if you take their teeth... "You're gonna die slowly ... Tooth Fairy!" His laughter held that high squeak that no rational person could ever attain. I knew that laugh well.

I crouched behind a sedan and closed my eyes. Taking deep breaths, I focused my awareness within. What was my body telling me? Sharp coolness drifted to my right. I turned to the right and tossed the knife over the hood of the sedan. The tear of steel into steel told me I had missed. However, I heard his quick shoes scuffle along the pavement. I missed, but not by much.

"Very good," it chuckled.

I could taste his bitter bloodlust and hatred. The demon's aura was a beacon of red. "Not very impressive, though. You don't hide very well." I moved to the other end of the car. My breathing nearly stopped, and my pulse was undetectable. The insides of my body were arctic. The dimness of the structure brightened as if someone turned up a dimmer switch.

The Virus was taking over.

I knew he was crouched on the other side of the car, just as I knew that he was aware of my location. There was no point in hiding anymore. We could both feel the battle.

We both wanted it.

We stood up. The demon's crimson eyes were two floating rubies in the darkness. His mouth opened in a twisted smile, displaying gruesomely long fangs.

"There was a Family in Indiana. Two years ago. Do you remember?"

"They didn't feel a thing. To tell you the truth, I didn't even look at their faces. I just staked and burned them." Their animalistic cries continue to reverberate in my head. They wailed long into the hours of the night. I could do nothing but listen to their screams.

His anger danced along my skin like an electric frostbite. "They were family! I was called to my Master the night before you killed them and took their teeth."

"Then come take your revenge!"

In a blur of movement, heralded by a war cry, the vampire jumped on the hood. A silver streak flashed in the darkness, tearing the fabric on my overcoat. I jerked back just in time to avoid a gash across my forearm.

The vampire waited for my next move. He favored his right foot. The left one caused a strong amount of pain. His right hand gripped the blade I left in his foot. The left arm hung at his side. It made me wonder how much it hurt digging silver metal from his shoulder. A wounded vampire was still dangerous. He was faster and stronger than I was.

"C'mon! Finish what you started." His eyes were filled with a festering hatred that was directed at me. He lunged forward with the knife. I dodged the thrust, but the vampire hit me with his shoulder, shoving the wind out of my lungs. My spine slammed against the edge of the sedan's roof. The force would have been enough to snap a normal man's spine.

I shoved my knives into the vengeful vampire's back. He howled as I raised my knee into his gut. I vaulted over my opponent in an awkward somersault. I fell off the hood and onto the concrete. The monster fell off the car too. We stood on rubbery legs. Blood poured from its wounds.

"Tell me about Dr. Worth." I gasped.

The monster spat blood at me. "No!"

"Why?" I yelled.

"To protect him." The vampire rolled onto his back.

"From whom?" I asked.

He chuckled. "*You.*" A tortured inhuman whose mission was to protect a human. That sounds familiar.

"Then why did you run away last night?"

He found interest in a Jeep Cherokee's rims and stared at them rather than me. "I-I was afraid ... of you." He shifted. The pain brought bloody tears to his eyes.

"What is so valuable about Dr. Worth?"

"I don't know. Valimus just told me to watch him. Kill me and get this over with."

"Not yet. Why is Valimus here?"

I was so wrapped up in unraveling this mystery that I did not see the fire behind his eyes. My victim screamed and pushed upward. He lifted me off the ground. His supernatural strength launched me off the pavement and hurled me into the ceiling. He screamed as he headed for the closest exit. As soon as my ears stopped ringing, I ran in hot pursuit. By the time I got to the exit and up the flight of steps, he pushed the exit door to go outside.

Into the daylight.

I tried to follow, but something compelled me to stop. I watched as the poor vampire burst into flames. He pirouetted, slapped at the flames that devoured his body, and stumbled into the street.

The loud horn of a semi truck signaled his end. The truck's hydraulic breaks screeched its protest. The semi slammed into the vampire, shattering him into a thousand flaming pieces. The demon's cries halted in mid-shriek. The streets were filled with the screams of onlookers as black ash rained down on them.

It started in the same place it ended, in a parking garage overlooking a building full of secrets. I knew before my job was done, I would open up the secrets in that building…even if it killed me. Little did I know just how close to death I was but saved by the hand of God.

Thank you, God, I whispered aloud with tears in my eyes as the clouds of my mind cleared.

Step Three

"Made a decision to turn our will and our lives over to the care of God as we understood *Him."*

The streets filled with the screams of onlookers as black ash rained down on them. My eyes traveled upward across the street to the Milton Center for Mental Health. A few gawkers in the building were looking downward, but one window in particular held my attention. From my spot in the entryway of the parking structure, I could see the worried look on Jack Worth's fat face.

He was in this up to his neck. It was my job to find out how deep he was in this mess.

Have you checked the classifieds lately? The Ancients were around for centuries and they were toying with my head. Why? Wasn't there anything on NBC? After walking two blocks west of the accident, I found a newspaper machine. I fed coins into the box and pulled out a new copy of *The Culver's Bay Gazette.* It took me precious seconds to flip to the classifieds section where I found a message waiting for me.

Gabriel,
"When the Indigo aura turns Midnight, the Evolution begins."

-V

Within the blink of an eye, the image of humans chained to a wall a groveling on a cool floor flashed behind my eyes. The dripping fangs of two familiar vampires snapped at me. The Baltimores! They were hurt and scared of some demon. There was a creature out there, and it was worse than the demons I was hunting. I refolded the paper and put it in one of my deep pockets. What was this game? What was this beast? The more I learned, the more pieces to the puzzle I found. Now, there was a new piece.

The police put up yellow crime scene tape. Cones were set up, blocking traffic in both directions. I stood among the other watchers trying to eavesdrop on what the police knew.

Worth headed for the parking structure across the street. He zeroed his angst on a plainclothes detective writing on a steno pad. "I've got to go. You've got to get this tape down."

"Sorry, sir," the detective said with a tired yawn. "This is a crime scene."

"The ramp? The frying guy got hit by a Mack truck out *here!*"

"But he was set on fire *in there.*" The detective hooked a thumb to the parking structure. "Hell, I don't even know why I'm talking to you. What did you see?"

"N-nothing." The good doctor vanished from the detective's sight.

I kept him in my sights as we made our way westward.

A block away, I watched him hail a cab. I sped my pace so he would not get away. The cab came to a halt by the time I reached him. He gasped as he felt my weapon prod him at the base of his spine.

"Speak or scream and I'll redecorate the inside of this cab with your intestines." I smiled.

Worth opened the door, nodded at me, and slid inside. I had no need to keep the Beretta in my hand, so I put it back at my waistband, and then shut the door behind me.

"Where to?" The driver, an older woman with gray hair, asked. "Just drive, please," I said.

"Any direction in particular?" She had a smoker's rasp.

"Eat up the meter."

"You got it," she said.

"Was that ... you?" the therapist asked me.

"Yeah," I growled the truth, "that was me."

"Wh-wh-what do you want?"

"Answers."

"I was told to go to those AA meetings the day you started showing up for them."

"By whom?"

"The couple." He didn't need to be more specific than that.

"Was there another ... person with them? Tall, slender, long hair?"

"Their Master," he said, nodding. He looked at the driver through the glass. "I saw him once. In the shadows." He paused then asked, "A-are you like them?"

"How did you find out about them?" I ignored his question.

"Winthrop. We both worked at Amhearst years ago. I was looking for an out, but Dave ... he ... he enjoyed working with the ... ah, convicts. All I wanted was to finish my residency and open a private practice. I could never understand Dave's passion."

His eyes grew haunted. "I-I ... saw him," he whispered. "He was in the parking structure. I thought he was with a girl he was cheating on Jessica with. But he looked at me with those eyes. They were purple! He hissed at me with-with these sharp teeth. Blood stained his whole mouth. I mean it looked like he was a ... a..." He was looking for a rational word to use.

I finished the thought for him. "Vampire."

Worth nodded. His mouth worked, but it took several tries before sound came from it. "He told me he could open up the world for me. He could help me start my practice and give me whatever I wanted.

28

"If I hadn't seen him kill with my own eyes, I wouldn't have believed a damned word he said. He talked of another, of beings that were of a higher evolutionary plane than ours. He said he could make me *one* of them."

"Why didn't you want it?"

"I remembered how he looked in that parking structure that night. It was the same structure where the vampire was just killed. The one *you* killed. I keep seeing his animalistic eyes, his long fangs, and the open lust of his kill." He swallowed hard. "I don't want to be like that." His voice was a whisper. "I don't want to be like that for an eternity. Eternity is a long time."

"Not as long as you'd think."

Seeing the threat, he continued. "We came to an understanding. We'd help each other out when we could. Dave ran Amhearst and I had a successful private practice."

"What happened?" I asked.

"Dave and I spent quite a bit of time together. I got to know him and Jessica well. When he disappeared, I felt it was my duty to make sure Jessica and Ryan, their son, were okay." I noticed the change in speed of his pulse. He was nervous when talking about them. He really cared about them. Either that or he was hiding something else. I wanted to ask how a vampire, especially a Master who had been around for several hundred years, could conceive a child.

They *were* evolving! Was this the evolution that the message foretold?

What if Ryan was the first *natural* vampire/human hybrid?

"About a month ago, this couple came to me. They told me they knew my relationship with some guy called Malfric. It wasn't until the conversation went on for a half an hour before I realized they were talking about Dave. They showed me what they were and threatened to kill me if I didn't do what they asked. So, I was told to keep tabs on you *and* the Winthrops. I want out of this. Just let me get on with my life. I'm no use to anyone. Now, you know all that I do."

"What about your research? What did you dig up?"

"Everything he has is connected to Amhearst. Not much info there." Jack sounded exasperated. "Please, Gabe. You know everything."

His words rang true in my ears. *Damn!* I thought. *Malfric must have kept his private records at home*. The weariness hit me like a hammer blow to the skull. I yawned and tried to make it look like boredom.

"If I find out you're hiding anything from me, death will be the least of your worries."

"Wh-wh-why do you care?" He shook like a leaf.

"It's my job," I told him. "Tomorrow, after the meeting, we meet and you tell me whatever you can dig up on Winthrop and his interest in Amhearst. Where do The Baltimores hang out?"

"I saw one of them with a matchbook from a club called The Darkness. It's a Goth club over on Averill." I told the driver to stop the car. Without a backwards glance, I shut the door and headed for the diner.

****

I scouted out the club well before I entered it. It was a two-story brick building that reminded me of a firehouse. The windows on the second floor were blackened out. There was a fire escape on the west side of the building and an exit door in the rear, which led to a small parking lot that was packed. The entrance in the front had a long line.

The clientele below added to its look. Most dressed in black, but black wasn't the only gothic color that these depressed humans wore. Reds, blues, and purples peppered the line. A lot of them had on leather; some sported pale makeup. Most of the women went for black lipstick and eyeliner. Some wore chains and studded collars. This was more than your simple Goth club of Anne Rice lovers.

I tasted their anticipation. It slid down my throat like warm honey and tasted of cinnamon. I savored its soothing properties as it coated the inside of my body, like a formless enti-ty. A pinprick of energy opened from a point below my navel. The power vibrated from within, turning into a cool breeze that filled me. That was the beginning of a supernatural sense. It was The Virus responding to a similar power nearby. The demons were waiting for me, but which ones? Was it the bloodthirsty couple from Tallmadge, or was it the evil entity that was stalking the city?

I kept my hands loose at my sides. The demons were faster and stronger than I, but they were arrogant. Being a preda-tor can have that effect. My thoughts returned to the vamp that underestimated me earlier that day. I felt a brief stab of its pure fury. *Keep focused, Gabe*, I chided myself.

While I made my way to the stairwell that led to the sec-ond floor, I palmed a silver blade. I wasn't happy with the shape of the throwing blades. Since they were in the shape of crosses, a blade could get snagged against my jacket sleeve or catch on a sheath. Diego and I needed to have a small talk about sacrificing efficiency for style. Diego was a young kid who lost his parents due to a vicious vampire attack. However, I was able to save him. He hung out with The East LA *Bandidos,* a hard-core gang in Los Angeles. Diego made weapons untraceable by filing off the serial numbers and played around with making knives. The kid was an artist. He even created the silver bullets I used. He told me they were hollow pointed 9mm rounds. The LA cops called them "Cop Killers" since they could travel through bul-letproof vests.

Silver bullets were his specialty.

As a result, my ammo and knives were untraceable. The gun, a Beretta 92-F, was taken from a cop I was unable to save several years ago.

The cackles of the Voices echoed, but I had the feeling that some of the Voices didn't belong to Council members. There was something in the Virus that links us. I wouldn't let that bond weaken me. I had to make it an asset.

Otherwise, I would be dead as soon as I crossed the threshold.

At the top of the stairs, a corridor led to multiple rooms. The din of the techno music receded behind the soundproof walls. A dark halo ringed the door at the end of the corridor. More laughter greeted me as I continued down the long hallway. Nine-millimeter silver sat in the magazine, waiting for action. As I approached the door, it opened. My finger tensed on the trigger.

"Please, come in, Mr. Brimstone." The familiar voice of Nathaniel Baltimore drifted back.

****

I passed beneath heavy purple curtains into a room where three of the four walls were covered in black paint. The other wall was brick. A nearly nude man and woman were chained to the wall. Large sofas ringed the room with couples lounging on them. Nathaniel and Miranda Baltimore looked so different from the last time I'd seen them. Normally, they were extras in a Norman Rockwell painting. I recalled their dispassionate gazes as they stared at me through a tiny window. Nate Baltimore had short blonde hair. Now, he wore his hair black and wavy. The loose curls drifted below his shoulders. His skin, paler than when I last saw him, nearly blended in with the white dress shirt opened to the middle of his chest. He had on black leather pants and matching riding boots.

Did Valimus force *all* of his followers to read Anne Rice?

Miranda, who dyed her hair a flaming red, wore a white peasant dress with a black upside down cross hanging between her cleavage, and black leather wrist straps wrapped around her. The Baltimores sat on a dark couch. Both of them patted servants who writhed on the floor below them.

I could not stop laughing.

The two guards who stood along the walls wearing black t-shirts and jeans growled at me. Their fangs dripped from thin lips. The vampires on the couch lost their malignant grins. They too bared their Virus-coated fangs.

I'd seen the vampire fantasy play out before a million times. Vampires who loved being part of the club scene enjoyed being around depressed, suicidal humans; they were easy prey.

Miranda hissed as she came off the couch. Without thinking, I fired a shot into her upper thigh. She crumpled to the floor. The soundproofed walls and the harsh techno music muffled the noises.

In less than a heartbeat's time, one of the vamp guards had my gun arm in his hands. He was ready to break it, but by that time, I had palmed a blade as soon as I shot Miranda. The guard left his throat exposed as I shoved the longest tip underneath the chin, a few millimeters above the Adam's apple. The blade was angled upward so it would travel behind the jaws and into the brain. The demon's eyes rolled into his head and his body shut down like a light switch.

The other bodyguard stayed crouched, ready to strike. The humans chained to the wall screamed. Most of them cowered to the floor, trying to look invisible. Two feet away, Miranda was cradled by her infected husband. Their eyes blazed with fire.

"Everyone keeps their cool and no one needs to die tonight." Well, no one *else*.

"H-h-hurts," Miranda cried. Crimson tears trailed down pale skin.

"I bet." I nodded my head.

"You will burn in the deepest caverns of Hell!" Out of the corner of my eye, I saw the demon bodyguard inch out of my line of sight. Without thinking twice, I shot it in the chest. The monster cried as it crumpled to the floor, renewing the screams of the humans.

I walked over to the cringing humans and demons and took a seat on one of the sofas. I bounced twice on the cushions and smiled. "Comfy."

"What do you want?" Nate Baltimore asked.

"You lured me across three state lines. Why don't you tell me?" I sat back and trained the Beretta on the couple.

"If my wife dies-"

"Your wife *is* dead. I gave you the option of letting her die a painless death. You chose to be one of Valimus' brood. You got your wish. It's time to pay the price."

"The Master will suck the marrow from your bones!" Miranda clenched her jaws as she gripped her wounded thigh. Blood seeped through her hand. Not very surprising; she had fed recently. I looked over at the humans who were chained to the wall. They dripped with fear. Déjà vu washed over me. The vision was coming true. That meant the demon was nearby. I looked around the room, waiting for it to show.

I shook the thoughts from my mind and returned to the task at hand. "The threats are getting boring. I'm starting to put the pieces together but help me along. Malfric lived here with a wife and son. Why? How was he able to impregnate a human?"

Miranda hissed at me.

I put a second bullet into her opposite thigh. When the echoes of the gunshot and screaming died down, I had to listen to Nate's cursing and vows to kill me in imaginative ways. Ignoring him, I continued my interrogation.

"What is Malfric's connection here?" I aimed the weapon at Miranda's left shoulder. "Before you say anything that would result in another shot, let me say that I've got seven more clips." I looked around the room for the monster, but it never came.

"We don't know!" Nate shrieked. "I swear, we don't know. Valimus found out Malfric was here so he told us to tail him. When he learned about his residency at the asylum and his friendship with the human, he told us to ... befriend him." The demon talked quickly. For a brief moment, I saw the fresh-faced kid full of fear who was worried about his injured wife.

Since Valimus was a rogue vampire targeted for elimination by The Council, the vamps sired by him would also be considered *persona non grata* by the Ancients. Malfric was a member of The Council, who was in charge of The Facility.

"What is Valimus doing here?" I relaxed into the sofa. The Beretta wasn't even pointed at them. The humans were statues. Their eyes riveted on us, and I could tell they did not understand a damned thing we were talking about.

Nathaniel smiled through jagged teeth. His amber eyes glowed. "When the Indigo aura turns Midnight, the Evolution begins."

"What does that mean?"

"Ours is not to question, half-breed. Ours is to do our Master's bidding." Baltimore's voice turned reptilian.

"You're hiding something." Another bullet whizzed through the air. It sheared off a major portion of Nate's left ear. He roared with pain as he clutched the portion of his ear still attached to his skull.

"When the Indigo aura turns Midnight-" he chanted.

"I know. I know," I interrupted with a wave of my hands. "Auras belong to beings, so you must be looking for a human. Who is it?"

"I don't know."

"Talk."

"I don't know!" Her voice quivered. "Please, don't hurt my husband. I-I…" she lowered her head. "I've hurt him enough already."

Miranda killed her husband that night by infecting him with The Virus. "I don't want to be without him. You can understand that, right?"

"No," I lied and aimed the Beretta between them. Miranda's face was a mask of pain. Nate's was filled with pure hatred. His hands gripped his ear, trying to stanch the flow of blood. All the hate and darkness that came from within me tensed my finger on the trigger. I came within a millisecond of killing them, but a large force pushed me to the ground. The weapon went sliding across the room.

The hulking vampire loomed over me like an imposing storm. His head was bald and it reflected the dark neon lights of the room. He wore a black t-shirt that would have ripped from his body if he'd flex his biceps. His eyes flamed with a brilliant ruby, the color of anger.

One second he stood over me with his tree-trunk sized arms wrapped across his brick wall of a chest. The next second he let out a roar and picked me up from the floor. His godawful cry smelled of dried blood and rotting flesh. Before I knew it, I was across the room on the floor, feeling an ache in my back.

"How the hell did I get over here?" I asked. When I looked up at the charging giant, I knew how.

The beast balled up my shirt and lifted me off the floor single handedly.

A meaty fist smashed into my skull; he pummeled me to the soundtrack of the techno music and the Baltimores' evil cheers and laughter. The world was a blur. The Voices in my head laughed along with the evil couple. I had to do something.

I had a silver dagger in my hand without thinking of where I drew it from, as if God himself placed it in my hand. The blade glinted a bright light that couldn't have come from any- where else but the Lord himself, blinded the beast. He staggered back. I put everything I had into the thrust and stabbed into the monster's neck until it hit bone. *Good luck prying that from your spine*, I thought. The demon choked on the weapon and lost all interest in me. Something inside of me told me to dive out of the way, which I did. Less than a second later, bullets from my Beretta riddled the monster that nearly crushed me. The Voices cried out in distraction, but they were drowned out by some- thing else ... a beautiful voice singing in Latin. Something told me that the song was a hymn.

The world was a blur, but I continued to dive again (this time to the left). More bullets whizzed past my head. The heav- enly music played in my mind again but this time, I saw a face. It was a beautiful woman who smiled at me. She looked so familiar. I was blinded but still running, still fighting. I gave myself over to the bright light, to God. God was a vengeful being. He saw what I was doing and guided me in the right direction. I knew this and for the first time in my life…I knew no fear. He would protect me, using this angel, who stood in the corner of the dark room radiating a bright light. Neither Nathaniel nor Miranda saw the angel in the corner. They weren't worthy of seeing her.

I grabbed another throwing blade and tossed it in the general direction of the shooter (or at least where I thought the shooter would be). Miraculously, I heard a scream and the heavy clatter of the weapon against the floor.

Slowly, the world came into focus. My eyes riveted onto the fallen Beretta, which I scooped up easily enough. I slipped in a new magazine and was back in control once again. With my body crushed and beaten to a pulp, I gasped for air and aimed at the married couple. I looked into the corner of the room where the angel was, but she was gone.

Good, I thought. *I don't want the angel to see this*. I aimed the weapon at Nate, but Miranda filled the front sight.

"Kill me if you must, but please, let my husband live." Once again, they became that scared couple in Ohio.

"I'm allowing you the opportunity to buy his life." I aimed the weapon at his face.

Her eyes leaked blood. "Culver's Bay sits on a cluster of ley lines. These are sources of power."

"No!" her husband screamed.

"I am saving your life," she cried to him. "The prophecy is to be fulfilled in a place of power. This must be the place. The Salem Witch Trials, Stonehenge, Area 51 … all of these places are atop clusters of ley lines. This is where it will begin." The tears flowed like a blood-soaked river. "Please let him live. You know all we know."

Because they gave me information, I would give them a reprieve. I had found my prey. I had found the monster.

And it was me.

I put away my gun and turned away.

"Y-y-you're not going to kill us?" Miranda looked confused.

"I still have a use for you."

Nate's eyes filled with suspicion.

"I want you to find out about that … passage … of Valimus'. What does it mean? We're going to keep that meeting tomorrow night at Meadowrest. If you don't show, or you don't have valuable info, then … well … you know the threat."

I headed for the door. When I had it open, the techno music drifted in. Before I could leave, I heard Miranda's voice. "We won't have the strength to take on Valimus."

"There are several warm bodies right here. Begin with them."

The demon is here, the Voices whispered to me. They were right.

I slammed the door behind me.

Then came the screams.

Step Four

"Made a searching and fearless moral inventory of our-selves"

Culver's Bay is a city where black ash rains along the streets and a prophecy can spill the blood of the innocent. This was the perfect place to find a monster. Last night, I found that monster, and clearly it was me.

The city hummed with a supernatural energy that I had never felt before. There was an inexplicable pull I felt towards Culver's Bay, a city that the locals affectionately called "The Bloody Bay." Little did I know it was the thing that drove me here. Thanks to my "interrogation" earlier that night, I knew what it was.

The *ley lines*.

Culver's Bay sits on a cluster of ley lines, Nathaniel Balti-more had told me. *These are sources of power.*

What kind of power? Was this what that prophecy the Voices were telling me about?

I gripped the copy of my Alcoholics Anonymous book and nearly tore it in half.

I could not remember why the streets rained ash the morning I went after the Baltimores. All I could recall was the gnashing teeth of a demon in a parking ramp. His hatred dripped onto me with the consistency of syrup, thick and malleable. As I continued to worry the copy of *The Book*, I tried to remember the feeling of acceptance and warmth I received when I first stepped into the AA meeting several weeks ago. When I first arrived in Culver's Bay, I found myself at a local YMCA. My eyes were riveted to the Alcoholics Anonymous flier near the front door. Something called me to the meetings. The more I learned about alcoholism, the more akin to the addicts I became.

I had forgotten about the head of the group, Hayes Sanders, who was sharing his ways of coping with his addiction. I also had forgotten that I was sitting in an uncomfortable folding chair in the basement of the YMCA. The smell of stale coffee, and even staler doughnuts, was long forgotten. How could I focus on the woes of my addiction when there were more pressing matters to attend to?

Yet, I could not even focus on that. The screams from the night before continued to haunt me. That previous night, I walked away from two vampires while they devoured innocent people. Sure, I was battered and bruised and nearly broken into pieces, but I should have done more, and I just didn't give a damn. Hayes' meaningless diatribe on addiction and booze was eclipsed by the howls, wails, and pleas of those unfortunate humans as the vampires opened up their bodies and sated themselves on the essence of their lives.

Jealousy! the Voices accused.

They were right. I wanted to be there to partake in the bloodletting. I yearned for hot warm, sticky fluids dribbling down my maw while I tore into their bodies with my sharpened incisors and claws.

Relish the pain! they taunted.

I was nearly drooling when Rachel took the seat next to me. "Hi, Gabe," she said as she took a sip of her weak coffee.

"H-h-hi," I stammered. I knew my face was ashen and my eyes bloodshot. I must've looked like I was going through withdrawal.

"Are you okay?" she asked.

I could not help but listen to the blood sloshing through her veins. The skin was a sensitive canvas. It would not take much strength to tear through it and feast on the warm insides. Her body sizzled with a heat unlike anything I have ever felt. She was feverish. An arctic chill rushed my body, causing her to shiver as well.

"Gabe, are you okay?" She looked around and realized that no one noticed my pain. She helped me out of my chair and we made our way out of the meeting.

My cheek rested against her shoulder. This was not making matters any better. The blood moved along her body like a tidal wave. Its roar was deafening.

"R-R-Rachel … please…"

"It's okay. You've got to get some fresh air. It's the cravings. You've got to remember the bad stuff. Remember the terrible jitters in the morning. Remember the…" She continued talking, but I was beyond listening.

She's taking you into the alley. No one will see her. No one will notice she is gone. Take her!

All that was decent and *human* in me fought against the Voices. It was all I could do to concentrate on Rachel's hands gripping my arms, trying to keep me on my feet. I had to focus on the present. To concentrate, I returned to my breathing. Maybe that would keep the Voices of the Masters at bay.

An instant later, I felt the cool night air tickling my body. It was slightly soothing. Before I knew it, I pushed Rachel against the grimy wall of the alley. My teeth extended and ready to sink into her flesh. My eyes bored into hers and I saw something disturbing, there was no fear in them.

"What the hell are you doing?" Her voice filled with steel. It was like my fangs weren't even there! Her eyes held a power within them that pushed my hunger away, but not too far. "Gabe, you can't let this beat you. I know what it's like to be strung out and to want a fix badly, but you are too valuable to let it beat you." She acted as if she never believed I was a vampire.

Sometimes people don't see what is right in front of them.

"I … I want … a … fix … badly." I stared at her throat. Tapping a vein would be easy.

She was fast. I never saw her hand, but it smacked across my cheek just the same. The sound filled the alley with a deafening clap. My mouth gaped open; I was dumbfounded. Then, I laughed. Rachel did too. It was a nice, normal sound. The last person that smacked me … well, let's just say it didn't end well for them.

"It's been a long time since I was smacked like that," I said between bouts of giggles.

"It's been a long time since I had to smack someone like that. And I can't say that they laughed afterwards." We leaned against opposite walls of the alley and looked at each other. I was the first to turn away. I knew she could see the bruises of my run in with the huge vampire the other evening. "Gabe, what happened? Are you in some sort of trouble?"

"Rachel, I-" *What're you going to say? You're a vampire hunter? You have an addiction to blood and that you go to AA because it's the closest thing to Vampire's Anonymous you're ever going to get?* I shook my head, pushing the Voices to the deepest recesses of my psyche. "I'm in trouble." Hey, at least it's the truth. "People are after me. I've been running for a long time."

"Moving from state to state doesn't get you any closer to who you are than you were in the last one." As if she slapped me again, I dropped my jaw. She smiled a grin that would've looked at home on someone thirty years her senior. "I know about these things. I've been running for a long time too."

"I'm just tired, you know?" I looked into the night sky, wondering what I expected to see. "I am a bad man. I did bad things. I lied, cheated, stole." Have I killed? Can you kill someone that was already dead? "I've used people." Is the addiction the monster, or does it make us a monster? I've spent my life hunting and killing monsters. What do I do when I have realized that I *am* the monster?

Then, Rachel asked a sobering question: "Did you do this while under the influence?"

I looked at her with tears brimming in my eyes. "I don't know anymore."

"Remember the prayer. 'God, grant me the serenity to accept the things I cannot change; courage to change the things I can; and the wisdom to know the difference.'" As she said those words, I said them along with her.

And it made sense.

I could not change the reality around me, but I *could* change how I reacted to it. I can make a difference; I can help others. I may be a monster, but that does not dictate that I should do evil. My eyes were downcast and I was deep in thought, so I did not notice that Rachel had stepped closer to me. She placed her arms atop my shoulders. Looking into her eyes, I saw the authenticity in them. She believed in beating this demon, this addiction. She reached out to hug me. It was that beautiful woman's strength that gave me enough resolve to push her to arm's length. She looked at me.

"Gabe, I don't understand."

"And I pray you never will." I strode from the alley; I knew what had to be done.

And I knew that I could do it.

****

It did not take me long to reach the cemetery. I wish it had. The extra time would have given me an opportunity to reflect on nearly killing Rachel. *The Book* was a great source of comfort for me. It reminded me that I had not failed. The best thing for me to do was walk away. But sometimes, walking away is the most difficult thing a person can do. I passed the test of my addiction. I was going to beat it.

I took a narrow pathway past Mike's fixed plot. I rounded a hill and saw two figures moving near a dying tree. When I put the car in park, the moving figures stood still and stared in my direction. I held the Beretta at my side.

The wind drifted the ends of the three-quarter length coat I wore. I passed the gothic-styled tombstones as I made my way to the undead couple. As I got closer, I could discern the grim features of the pale vampire duo. Miranda wore a purple corset and a long black velvet skirt. Her dark hair cascaded down her back and her eyes glinted evil rubies that lit up a piece of the darkness. Nathaniel wore a pair of black leather pants and a lacy white shirt. I shook my head as I stood within five feet of them.

"Still playing to the stereotypes? What're your names now? Carmilla and Lestat?"

Nate hissed at me, baring long razor fangs as he fell into a fighter's crouch.

"Please spare me the melodramatic garbage. It gets tiresome fast." I aimed the Beretta between them. The couple shivered at the sight of it. The promise of deadly silver cutting through their bodies kept them humble. "I let you live because I wanted to get information. Please tell me I did the right thing."

Their slow smiles sent alarm bells ringing in my thick skull. I should've known I was walking into a trap, but my mind wasn't where it should have been. I couldn't stop thinking about Rachel. The pain I felt watching her with Hayes was worse than a gunshot through the kneecap. And believe me; I *know* what that feels like.

Pure instinct saved me from a serious eye-gouging by a whispering kill that took a swipe at me. The laughter of the undead echoed in the cooling night. The demons' claws burned deep scratches into the right side of my face. I fell into a roll and moved across the soft grass.

Another creature seemed to fall from the sky towards me. I rolled away from the demon. Its feet hit the soft earth where my head used to be. I fired the Beretta from where I lay on the ground. The first round entered just below the chin and traveled through the top of his skull. The second bullet tore a large hole through his throat. I could see the Adam's apple explode. The vampire crumpled next to me. Its body twitched a few times before it was still.

I rolled to my feet and took a kneeling stance. I was sighting in on Nathaniel Baltimore when a semi truck slammed into me from behind. Well, at least it *felt* like a semi. The vampire that hit me from behind laughed before he gave an inhuman yell. *Never celebrate before the game's over,* I thought as I palmed a throwing knife from my jacket.

I was lying prone on the grass. By the time I turned over onto my back, he was trying to sink his fangs into my throat. My forearm was braced across his neck. Long, dripping fangs gnashed together. Its saliva drooled onto my shirt.

"I'm gonna tear your heart out!" As soon as it finished its statement, I shoved the cross-shaped throwing knife between his teeth. The demon did what I expected: he clamped down. By the time his teeth ground together, my hand had pulled away from his mouth. Blood splashed out of the sides of his face as the cross points protruded from his cheeks. The monster screamed and rolled off me. I pawed around the grass until I found the Beretta and put two 9mm Parabellum hollow points into his chest.

"You did this to us!" The screeching banshee wail was followed by a female vampire rushing at me. I did not recognize any of the demons that attacked me, but I recalled her.

She was chained to the wall of the club from last night.

These were the poor souls I refused to save that night.

The demoness was right. It *was* my fault.

Knowing I didn't have enough time to aim, I stroked the Beretta's trigger twice. One bullet sheared off her left ear. The second one sheared away the right side of her jaw. The banshee wailed even louder as she stumbled. I grabbed her by the collar and aimed her into the direction of a cross-shaped tombstone. Her screams turned to moans after she smashed through the tombstone. The vampiress fell onto her face and rose to her knees moments later. She turned to look at me. Her hiss was full of hate. Blood and fragments of the broken memorial spilled from her ruined mug. I felt bad about what I did to her head.

So I shot her in the face.

I reloaded the weapon.

Four other vamps stood around the soft hill where I perched. The Baltimores were standing nearby, waiting to pounce on me. The world came to a screeching stop. Four vampires ringed the hill with two more standing mere feet away from me.

"Who wants to die next?" A small throwing blade slipped from a wrist sheath and into my free hand.

"They are eager to bathe in your blood," Miranda said with a sadistic grin.

It was hard to take her seriously when she looked like a character from a gothic romance novel.

"They wanted to play vampire; now's their chance. I didn't tell them to offer themselves to you. Besides, I wasn't the one who infected them." The four demons looked from me to the Baltimores.

"He should have saved you!" Nate yelled. He pointed a slender, sharp fingernail at me.

"Why?" I asked. "Do you see an 'S' on my chest? I'm not into the hero racket. I don't save lives. I just take them."

"Why don't you attack?" Miranda shouted.

"Because they are just like me." I growled at her as I moved towards them. The Beretta was at the ready, held at the hip. "They are not sure who the 'bad guys' are." My laugh was genuine. I bathed in the irony. "They have realized that the romantic gothic picture that you have painted was a mere illusion. They have seen the curse of The Nosferatu Virus!"

The undead creatures closed in on the couple. Fear drifted from them in waves that rippled the reality around us. It massaged my senses, but agitated the feral beasts that closed in. "You have seconds to tell me what you know."

Baltimore screamed and tried to attack. So I pumped a silver bullet into his thighs. The male Baltimore swore loudly and fell onto his side. *Déjà vu!* I thought. He clutched his ruined legs and let out a wild howl. His wife ran to his side and, once again, clutched him to her breast. He continued to scream, staring at me through pain filled eyes.

The demons nearby inched closer. The fresh scent of blood drew them.

"The beasts!" Miranda cried. "Keep them back! What are they? Th-th-they're not … us."

"Sure they are," I smiled. "You decided to turn innocent people into the undead but did not teach them how to control the Thirst."

"For God's sake, help us!" Nate's voice was tempered with hysteria. "We-we'll tell you everything."

I fired a shot into the night sky. The roar pushed the demons away, but only for a moment. "I've bought you some time. Talk or I'll give these things a feast to remember."

"Valimus has his eye on someone here for the prophecy," Miranda said.

"Tell me something I don't know!" I smiled at the feral vamps; then, I tucked the Beretta into my wide jacket pocket. This gave them a bit more confidence. They inched closer to the vampires. "You'd better do it quickly."

"Malfric! Valimus is looking for Malfric!"

I watched the ravenous vampires tear at the undead couple to shreds. The smell of blood and torn flesh blossomed outward. The feral vampires gathered around them and fed.

Do it!

Do it!

Do it!

With a dark growl, I pushed the vampires aside and stared at the bloody couple. Nate was in the worse condition. Slashes and bites covered him from head to toe. The Baltimores looked up at me with pain filling their eyes. Miranda raised a hand towards me. Her pitiful eyes transfixed on my blank face.

"P-p-please…" She hissed.

Amid the tearing and devouring that the rabid monsters were doing to her husband, I paused and looked at the beautiful Miranda Baltimore. I reflected on the ramifications of indulging in my addiction, or falling from the wagon. My mind returned to my conversation with Rachel. I was running from something and running *towards* something at the same time. My therapist had said that to me on multiple occasions. Deep down I knew I was a monster, yet I am a monster hunter. Does that mean that to be successful, I must kill myself? I have thought of that many times in the dead of night, looking out the window of my room at the bright silvery orb that hung in the sky and drove people like me insane.

I couldn't stop seeing Rachel's concerned face in my mind's eye. They wouldn't stop pleading with me. But that didn't stop me.

I tore into her and continued to feed as the others ripped at her husband with renewed abandon.

I failed.

And it felt so good.

Step Five

"Admitted to God, to ourselves, and to another human being the exact nature of our wrongs."

She was running through the dark claustrophobic night-mare. The labyrinthine hell of steel and brick intertwined with steel tubing. She could see in the dark. They could all see in the dark. However, that did not dampen her fears. The hounds of hell were nipping at her heels. They were coming.

They were coming!

Cornered.

Her breath came in ragged gasps. Yes, they could breathe. They didn't need to, but for the newly Turned, it was an instinctive reaction. It seemed like the normal thing to do.

She was far from normal. She was dead, but she was going to get deader if she slowed down.

The pace was hard to keep with the knee-deep water. She sloshed through it as fast as her slim legs would take her. Her mind told her that she was tired, even though it could have pushed on indefinitely.

Please, help me! her mind cried.

The sounds of multiple assailants growling and splashing feet drew ever nearer … nearer … nearer.

****

The vision vanished as violently as it appeared. The images were snapshots of someone else's terror. The daydreams had been pursuing me all day. It was the same thing: a woman in a sewer being chased by something. Whatever it was, it was many and hungry.

Returning to the present meant returning to my own problems. My biggest one occurred last night. When you fall off the wagon, one of the first things you're supposed to do is contact your sponsor. For me "falling off the wagon" meant nearly draining a vampire of her blood and leaving her and her husband to suffer at the hands of blood-crazed vampires.

Who would've thought that there'd be no chapter in our Book about that one?

So I sat in a 50's-styled diner and tried to drown my sorrows in strong black java, but it did not make me feel clean.

Not many things made me feel clean these days, even in the sterile conditions in which I find myself. I nursed the coffee Flo sat in front of me. "It's on the house," she said with a sympathetic smile.

I must've looked as bad as I felt. There's nothing worse than falling off the wagon.

Focus on the mission, I thought. *Don't dwell on the failure.* Take each day at a time, The Book tells us.

From my jacket pocket I pulled out a driver's license. It belonged to a man I buried, screaming but undead, in a Nevada desert years ago. His name was Winthrop. He was the director of a mental institute named Amhearst.

I knew him as a bloodsucking fiend named Malfric.

His license led me to this town, a town filled with shadows and humming with a magic that was threaded throughout the pavement, in the midst of its urban soul.

I remembered the look on her face when I sank my fangs into Miranda Baltimore's neck. The look of surprise was the most horrible part of it all. It was like I was betraying her. This game of cat and mouse I've been playing with them had rules.

As of late, I have been breaking them. Usually, I was the "good guy" and they were the "bad guys." I would find out their schemes and try to foil them like some Saturday morning cartoon. Lately, however, I have not been such a good guy. I'm not sure where I fall in the hero/villain categories. A hero would not have left humans to die in a club populated by the undead. A hero would not let his archenemies be torn apart, much less join in and help to kill one of them.

I never pretended to be a white knight, but I never thought I was a killer.

Until now.

Even though they are already dead, do I "kill" them?

"Are you okay?" The familiar voice came from behind me. I turned around in my booth to find Rachel standing near the entrance with concern written across her face. "What happened? Y-you freaked out back at the meeting."

I didn't mean to, I thought. I nearly attacked her in the alley of the YMCA where we held our AA meetings two days ago. I expected the Voices to chime in but they did not. My mind was still. Why?

Before I could think of possible reasons, the goth girl slid in the booth across from me. I continued sipping on my coffee. I was hoping it would buy me some time, but the expectant look on her face told me she knew the stalling game I was playing. Addicts must play that game a lot. "I ... I was getting an urge. When I haven't ... drunk ... and I need to, I get angry. Rachel, I'm not a nice person."

"No one who is craving a drink is a nice person. They want that drug more than anything and are willing to do anything to get it."

Even kill? I wondered. Looking out the plate glass window, I mostly saw the reflection of the rest of the diner. The fluorescent lights made it difficult to see the darkness beyond the window. But I saw a glimmer of a pale figure standing on the opposite side of the glass.

Valimus!

My hand gripped the Beretta beneath my jacket with ease. My body tensed.

"What is it?" Rachel gasped at my sudden reaction. "Gabe, it's just your shadow." My prey faded away from the window, replaced by my gaunt, pale features. It was so subtle, it made me wonder... "Gabe?" Her voice intruded my dark thoughts.

"Huh? Oh, uh … I'm … I'm sorry about last night." I stared at my reflection in the murky depths of the black coffee.

"I can feel that you're holding something back. The last thing you want to do is get in the habit of keeping secrets. It feeds into the addiction."

She was right. The greatest power of vampires wasn't their ability to live forever or their quick healing skills, but the fact that they have convinced mankind they do *not* exist. This secret makes them so powerful. It allows them to hunt *among* their prey. Movies where they take their victim into the shadows, kill them, and dissolve into mist were stuff of legend and bad Saturday night viewing. Why would they need to dissolve when they can walk out of the shadows among people who look like them?

"You are right. I have been keeping secrets, and yes, they do feed into the addiction, the monster, that I have."

"Monster?" Her voice was small. Her smile was even smaller. "I kinda like that. It's so … accurate." Flo sat a cup of unleaded in front of her. "It scares me too." Her electric eyes crackled.

It was easy to look away, to look at anything and everything except those eyes, her small nose, and her rosy cheeks. I nodded, "It's a way for me to conceptualize my issue. I feel like I need that. It's my way of dealing with it … the monster." For a moment, my mouth wouldn't work. My jaw just bobbed. Then, it started working again. "It's alive; you know my need. It ebbs and wanes like a tide in a storm. Sometimes I feel like I'm surfing on it. It's like, on my best … nights … I-I can ride it. I'm on top of it and I've got a lock on it. Then…" I rocked back and forth in my seat and wringed my hands. "Last night was difficult. I wanted a … drink … so badly." For the first time in about five of the longest minutes of my life, I looked up into her eyes. "I fell off the wagon." Tears brimmed in my eyes. Rachel's measured gaze was expectant. She was guarded and waited for me to continue. "After our discussion outside the Y, I was weakened. I went to Mike's grave with a bottle and I drank." It wasn't actually what happened, but it was close enough. I thought of my fangs sinking into Miranda Baltimore. Her tainted, black blood crashed through the back of my throat, coating the inside of my mouth with her life. I knew that was where the visions I had of the panicking vampires running through the sewers had come from.

When I noticed her intense gaze, I stopped reflecting. I stared back and the world went still, silent. Her eyes were chips of flint. I returned the look, but she never looked away. "How did you feel when you did it?" When I opened my mouth to speak, she interrupted me. "Don't lie to me. How did you feel?"

She was right; I was tempted to lie, to tell her how bad it tasted. "It was like a taste of heaven. Everything seemed perfect and the first drop was unlike anything I have ever felt before." My body trembled at the exquisite thought. I coughed and tried to compose myself.

"How did it make you feel after the relapse?"

Once again, I saw Miranda's look. She looked confused, afraid, and betrayed. "Horrible. I-i-it was indescribable." Looking into the dark depths of my coffee, all I was able to see was … me. "For years I've never had to account for my actions to anyone. That night I realized that I did have to account to someone. Me."

"And God." Rachel's words were of little comfort.

"God," I spat as I drained the cup. "Sometimes I'd like to get my hands on God." I put the cup on the table and Flo refilled it with a dead smile. "'Exact nature of our wrongs', huh?"

"Yeah." She smiled.

"If you only knew." It was meant to be a whisper, but she heard it.

"Knew what?" Her eyes narrowed.

"The extent of what I have done." I expected her to do something more than what she did. I expected her to look horrified, to ask what it was that I did, to reel back in disgust ... anything except for what she had done. Realistically, I knew I could never admit the exact nature of my wrongdoings. To do so would be selfish. Sure, I could unburden my soul to her, but that would introduce her to a world from which she could never return. It would mean opening her eyes to a reality that she knew from novels, fantasies, and cheap B-grade horror flicks. She wasn't ready for that kind of knowledge. No one would be. So, yes, I expected something other than her placing her hand atop mine.

When she reached out and touched my hand, which lay on a paper placemat, a powerful heat radiated outward and drifted along my body. The heat was overwhelming. I jerked my hand back and pressed my back against the booth. The beautiful gothic woman lowered her head.

"S-sorry. I ... I didn't mean..." She stepped from the booth and hurried from the diner.

Heat drifted from her body, like the trail of a comet. It was invisible to the human eye, but I saw it. It hovered around her, causing the air to shimmer as it does when looking at freshly laid asphalt at a distance during a hot summer afternoon.

Stay away! the Voices cried out. My vision blurred and blood seeped from my ears. I staggered from the booth.

"Gabe? Are you okay?" Flo's voice came back muffled.

****

She was hiding among the piles of trash in an alleyway. She sweated fear into the sacks of refuse and discarded food. She was cornered. The high bricked walls of neighboring buildings closed in on her. Wild eyes scanned the shadows. The darkness was a dim shade of gray for her. The fact that she could see into the darkness did nothing to stop her fright.

She could hear them.

Cornered.

Their terrible growls and savage panting echoed in the alley. The victim held her breath even though she was unaware of the fact that she had stopped breathing ten minutes ago. Something blurred by her, disturbing a sack of garbage that shivered against her face. The weight of the garbage was strangely comforting. It shielded her from the demons that stalked her.

Almost there, she thought. *I'm almost there.*

A wound at her neck opened up. More blood seeped from it. The sounds of growls and ripping of trash bags with razor sharp claws grew.

Almost there.

Where was she going? What would protect her from the bloody savages that had picked up her scent and followed her into the urban nightmarish hell of the downtown streets of Culver's Bay?

****

Another vision of Miranda Baltimore. I could feel her fear. It was like slipping into a pair of broken in shoes. Her feelings were complicated. Amid the fear and horror, there was a profound sorrow. She had lost her husband to the same creatures that were coming for her, stalking her, terrorizing her. *What is this game?* I wondered. The Voices were quiet. Was this another one of The Council's tricks? The stinging rays of pelting water washed the blood from my body. I watched the crimson swirl circle the drain with grim fascination. The cuts and bruises brought renewed pain once the jets of water hit me, but I did not mind.

When I stepped from the shower, the mirror was covered in fog. I wrapped a towel around my waist, exited the bathroom, and sat on the bed.

I leaned back against the headboard and reminded my-self of my next move: Amhearst. It had to be my next target. The asylum was a house of secrets.

"What's happening to me?" I whispered to the empty room.

A light but steady rain drifted across the cityscape. This industrial nightmare of Culver's Bay's downtown district was depressing. I focused my attention on the image I cast in the dark shadow. My pale, thin chest was a crisscross of scars from earlier wars with the undead. My face was freshly shaved. It would alter my appearance only slightly, but every little edge helped. I could not help but notice how sunken in my cheeks looked and how empty my eyes were.

I was a maniac.

I was not sure how long I looked in that window. It was long enough for me to reflect on the lives I had destroyed fighting this war. Each time I drove a silver blade through the heart of a demon, I destroyed a life. Every single time I pulled the trigger, sending 9mm silver slugs through the body of a hap-less soul, I destroyed a life.

Nathaniel Baltimore.

Jeanette Mullray.

Mike L.

Rachel.

The list was long so I must have been at the window for at least an hour. The urgent knocks on the door caused my heart to skip a beat. *Who could it be?* No one knew my location. The torn, bloody, and battered body of Miranda Baltimore stood in the doorway. "You!"

The vamp opened her mouth to speak, but blood poured from it. Her shaky legs gave out from under her. If I had not reached out to grab her, she would have fallen across the threshold. I carried her to the bed and grabbed a knife I had lying on the nightstand.

When I took a closer look at the beautiful demon, I saw multiple fang marks across her face. A chunk of flesh was taken from her left hip. She reeked of sewage and exhaustion.

"P-please … don't … let … them … get … me." The pleading in her eyes was hard to watch. She shivered, not from pain, but a fear so deep, it was primal. She was the fox who was afraid of the hounds. Her soft, glassy eyes were beyond pain. She felt a dark numbness.

I'd seen that look in her eye before. It was on a deserted stretch of dark road a few years ago. Miranda's blood, once again, spilled from her, flowing freely on the pavement. Her husband was next to her, trying to stem the flow. The past and present blended together in a cacophony of bloodshed that bordered on the fantastic.

Tears drooled down the sides of her face when she shook her head. "I h-h-hid in the sewers. They … chased me. They are hungry … been running." The vampiress worked her mouth for nearly a minute before more words came out. "Sh-should've … listened. Should've let you … k-k-kill-" A horrible coughing fit forced more seductive fluid from her lips.

She let the Virus infect her. This was her fault. I stared at her, thinking back among those I have killed. As many people as I have executed, I have never felt so afraid to watch someone die as I did that night. It was hard to look into her eyes. They were the eyes of the timid fox. Any other time, I would have reveled in the agony and fright.

Those luminous eyes faded away, then returned to me. "J-j-just wanted my husband. All I wanted was to … to … spend e-eternity with him." I strained to hear her words. "Did you ever wonder … why he spared Nate?" The thought of why Valimus spared her husband's life and not hers had only crossed my mind once.

"Why?" My voice was gentle.

"He does not Kiss anyone who would not make a good vampire. He knew Nate would … would f-fall." She coughed.

"I just wanted him."

Our heads turned to the door. The dying vampiress became stiff as a corpse. My hand gripped the steel of the throwing blade until blood dripped from my hand. The living dead shuffled outside the motel room. The starved vampires from the cemetery had followed their meal to my doorstep. They had been stalking her through the sewers for over twenty-four hours, and they were hungry. Their pitiful wails brought shivers throughout my body. Moments afterwards, their wailing was joined by scratching on the door. It would not take them long for the bloodthirsty demons to break in. I stripped the towel from my waist and put on my black slacks. Then, I pulled on my overcoat and drew the Beretta from my deep jacket pocket.

"B-b-brim…s-st-" she began.

"Don't talk."

"H-h-have to. Valimus knows who to Kiss to make the prophecy come true."

That got my attention. The pounding of the vampires grew farther away. "Who is it?" I sat by her side. With the quickness of a coiled cobra, Miranda's arm snaked outward and grabbed my jacket. "Amhearst…" Her life was fading away.

"Amhearst is a *cover* for the Facility? There's a new Facility, isn't there?"

She shook her head. "He was afraid … what you did with Malfric. He has Touched the mind of Malfric. He's insane … crazed by the Lust … all fear you." She rolled her eyes to the door. The scratching claws on the cheap wood mingled with the sickly moans of the undead things. "He is like them now." The scratching and pounding grew in its severity. I heard the wood begin to crack. When her cold hand reached out and clamped onto my forearm, I stared back at her. "It's all … a … a…" More thudding and cracking wood pulled me towards the door.

I aimed the gun at the door, which continued to shiver under the repeated blows of the ravenous vampires. "We need to get out of here … and fast." When I looked down at Miranda, I knew she was in no condition to go anywhere. My pulse thudded in my head.

Where will you go, Brimstone? The Voices taunted.

"Shut up!" I screamed. "Get out of my mind, you sons of bitches!" I was alone. The Voices, they were everywhere! I looked around.

"Not them ... it's him." She coughed up blood. "N-n-never them. V-val-"

Reality shivered as the blood-crazed monsters continued to break into the room. "Do ... do you mean that-"

"N-no ... Council. All a lie! J-j-just ... y-y..."

"Valimus!" More pounding at the door. "You bastards!" I screamed as the door began to splinter. Bits of wood broke from the door. The nearby window was still intact. How long would that last? Just by the wailing, I calculated three of them, the same number of ravenous creatures from last night.

Using a standard double-handed grip, I aimed at the crumbling door. I became all too aware of the bleeding woman in my bed. Most of the bed was black. The blanket atop the mattress was sticky. The coppery scent drowned out all my other senses. *Focus!* I told myself. *Don't think ... about ...* Miranda's supple neck sported several pairs of deep bite marks. Some of them were mine. The wounds just started to clot. The crusting blood begged to be licked off. When I noticed Miranda gazing at me, I became embarrassed. I returned my gaze to the zombies breaking down the door. Movement at the window drew my attention.

A graying undead being pressed against the window. The thing blinked at me. Its milky white eyes lacked any emotion or feeling. The flimsy door buckled. My hands shivered. The weapon strayed. Sweat dripped into my vision, blurring the nightmare/reality before me. They were ravenous, mindless creatures who would not listen to reason. These were the true monsters.

One glance down at Miranda told me death was coming for her. The exhaustion and blood loss were taking their toll. The bloodthirsty creatures outside the door could smell her death. They didn't just want her blood. They wanted her flesh. They wanted to tear her limb from limb and devour her.

And I was the entrée.

My body trembled as a chill filled me from the inside. The groans of the undead were urgent. Need eclipsed reason. A fist smashed through the door, but the odd angles of the fingers told me that it did not feel pain. It had a need so strong that it superseded the pain it was supposed to have felt. Splinters of wood stuck in its gray fingers and knuckles. It clawed at the door, tearing a fingernail right from its pinky.

Cornered.

The window smashed inward. The undead creature began to climb through the window. A shard of glass stabbed into its stomach and back. It smiled when it noticed us in the room. The creature opened its mouth in a twisted smile; a long, wet tongue lolled between the cracked lips. Fluids too thick to be saliva drained from the wet meat.

"Foooooooood," it croaked.

Step Six

"Were entirely ready to have God remove all these defects of our character."

"G-go." I barely heard Miranda's plea.

"What? I can't do that."

"Must..."

"I'm sorry. I promise to make amends for what I have done." The window cracked just as the door did. A newly made hole showed two vampires, both of whom tried to kill me the night before.

"I'll hold them off." Her voice was weak, but the resignation was as loud as a gunshot fired at point blank range.

"The hell you will!" I fired at the zombie in the window. Three bullets removed nearly half its skull, but the damned thing continued climbing into my motel room. *You're losing control!* the Voices mocked. *They will kill you and the betrayer.* "I know it's you, Valimus. There was never any Council! There were never any overseers. It was only you ... you and your minions." I continued to fire and curse the demon for his deception. *That may be true, but you still have lost control.* His laughter filled my head.

"God, grant me the Serenity to accept the things I cannot change, the Courage to change the things I can, and the Wisdom to know the difference." Those were the words Hayes Sanders stated in my mind. It was our Prayer.

The Prayer of the Addict.

It is too late! Valimus screeched in my head. *You cannot stop the inevitable. The prophecy will be fulfilled and there is nothing you can do about it. You are swinging at windmills, Quixote! There is nothing that can be done. Not even God can help you now, if He even would.*

Was I the lesser of two evils to Him? Would he see me through this, or would he let me die at the hands of ravenous zombies? At the time, I had no idea what that answer would be. At one point in my life, I thought I was doing the righteous thing. I thought I was doing God's work by vanquishing the hordes of the undead. I had thought that the voices I was hearing were the words of the Lord himself. When I found out I was just a hitman for a vampire, I knew that my life had little meaning. And even with all of that, would God still look favorably on me? Did He see me as a monster?

I thought of this as two zombie-like creatures tore through the door. They sniffed the air. Their once pathetic wails turned into agitated cries. One of the two vampires through the door recognized me. "You!" it screeched. It moved erratically, and a glinting piece of metal at the end of a silver chain slipped from a tear in his shirt. At one time the monster was a man; not only that, but he was a religious man. A cross swung from his neck. His gaping mouth was stained bloody red. Worms poured from a hole in his chest. I was guessing I had given him that one.

The least I could do was finish what I started.

I stroked the Beretta's trigger twice. Both hit the target, but not where I wanted them to go. The demon was moving faster than I anticipated. The first round cleaved his left ear off. The second one hit high on his chest. By the time I corrected my aim, he hit me with a flying tackle. The handgun skidded across the floor as we landed in a heap on the threadbare carpet. My hands were locked around its throat. I wasn't trying to strangle it. You can't strangle something that does not breathe.

The thing in my arms opened its foul-smelling maw. What was left of its lips curled upwards into a grotesque grin.

"Take a good look at your future." It laughed with a hellish cackle.

In my peripheral vision, I saw the nearly headless zombie crawling towards me. It left a smear of blood in its wake. Most of its face was gone, but the mouth and lower jaw were still intact. Viscous fluids drooled down the chin. It, too, smiled and waggled its dangling tongue in my direction.

There was one zombie left, and it was headed straight for Miranda. I needed to end this quickly, but this monster had fed. It was strong, and I had not drunk enough blood. I was the weaker man. I felt his teeth closing in on me. The zombie cackled like a jackal. "You will lose, Brimstone!" Its breath reeked of flesh and blood. I needed to free one hand to get to a throwing blade in my pocket, but that would have left me vulnerable to the other vampire.

Miranda Baltimore's ear shattering scream filled the room. The lone zombie must have gotten to her. The claustrophobic motel room filled with the overwhelming odor of blood. The zombie atop me and the near headless thing on the floor were distracted. I had the perfect opportunity to strike.

My body was weak; sleep deprivation, emotional turmoil, and delusions implanted by Valimus had drained most of me. However, I when I felt the vampire's metal cross touch my right cheek, I felt something foreign, but powerful, course through my veins. It allowed me to use the last reserves of supernatural energy I had to brace the monster up while I let go of him with my right hand. "Give me the courage…" I prayed through gritted teeth. A power that felt all too different filled my insides. I reached into my pocket and grabbed the knife. The longest tip of the four-pointed weapon stabbed into his body, just below the belly button. The vampire-like zombie howled. He had forgotten all about the ravenous beast eating the now dead vampire and slashed his claws into my locked arm. I reveled in his cries of agony as he struggled against my grip. When I started to yank upward, his screams increased. I fought to keep my grip around his throat as I slashed up. The blade cut into his stomach. His intestines spilled out onto me. Blood drenched the lower half of my body, pushing me further down a corridor of insanity. "...to change the things I can!"

When the zombie went limp, I tossed the disemboweled body to the side. The nearly faceless monster crawled towards the corpse, whose eyes fluttered open. The zombie looked over at the faceless thing and let out a godawful scream before it began chewing on the gory contents that trailed from his gaping wound.

Once I got to my feet, I stared at the horrible tableau on the bed. The zombie on the bed chewed at the heart of Miranda Baltimore, who stared at me through glassy eyes. Her body was torn in half at the waist. Her weak fingers moved slightly.

"I'm sorry." I spoke the truth. "I'm sorry ... for everything." Calmly, I walked across the room and picked up my gun. I waited until Miranda closed her expressive eyes before I shot her in the head. After that, I put a bullet into the mindless heads of the two living dead fiends.

A silence descended over the slaughterhouse. Looking around the room filled me with euphoria. The blood, the death, the bodies, the blood...

THE BLOOD!

I closed my eyes and took a deep breath of the wondrous odor. "God, grant me the serenity to accept the things I cannot change." I placed the warm, bloody cross against my forehead.

Revel in the massacre! Valimus shrieked at me. *Drink! Drink! Drink!* My body shuddered as saliva filled my mouth. I was so thirsty. The temptation was overwhelming. Instead, I walked to the closet, where I kept my bag full of clothes and gear and reached inside. I found the satchel of teeth and pliers with ease. The rage of what they had done ... what *he* had done ... took over me. With delicious brutality, I yanked the fangs out of the undead monsters' heads. The sickening crunch of giving bone soothed my anger.

"Yours will be the last teeth I snatch," I vowed to the demon inside of my head. I grabbed my gear and stuffed the pliers and bag of teeth inside. I headed for the door but stopped when I heard a pitiful sound. It was a cry that chilled me to my bones.

I ran back to the side of Miranda Baltimore and watched as her life slid from her feeble grip. My eyes were wide; I could not help staring into the hole in her skull.

"F-f-find … R-R-Richard Sto … Sto … Stoker." Her smile was haunting. "You will find everything … and it will destroy him and … you." The last word slid out of her mouth along with her life.

Silence filled the room with overwhelming deafness. The room grew still. As soon as I gathered my wits about me, I fled from the motel room. Out in the parking lot, I found the Cavalier I had stolen.

****

Darkness hung like a dead man from a weathered tree. It clung to my skin with the consistency of fresh honey. I wrapped myself in it and wore it like a worn glove. It felt familiar … like home.

I had been standing outside the building on the fire escape for about an hour. Was it really an hour since the gruesome events that have burned a hole into my mind? Was it an hour or a decade? Time lost all meaning for me. Seconds, minutes, hours, days…all of it slipped from my grasp like a slippery eel. I would try to understand them, but I just could not. As a perpetual insomniac/vampire hunter, I thought of time as "night" and "day." And in the dead of night, I stared through the window as my prey moved inside.

I always savored the hunt. Just like the demons I hunt, I relish the stalking just as much as the kill. Maybe that's why I am so good at it. Maybe that was why it took the authorities so long to catch me. *Remember the prayer*, I thought. As easily as the thought came to me, it was long forgotten. The part of me that was human was fading away, something that was easier and easier to do with each passing day. The darker part of me was surfacing. The part of me that enjoyed the hunt began to rule who I was.

The vampiric side of me was gaining more control.

Even though I was cognizant of what was happening to me, there was nothing I could do to stop it. As I stared at my prey, plotting the kill, I knew I should not do it. I knew it was wrong to take the life of a human. I did it once, and I had no desire to do it again … well, the human side of me had no desire to do it.

The monstrous side of me was another story.

My hands pressed against the glass of the window, watching my prey move about the apartment. The glass hummed with the vibrations of the victim's energy.

I felt my fangs press against the insides of my mouth, threatening to tear it to shreds. Pressing against the window, I was able to raise it.

It's unlocked! the Voice in my head screamed. *Go for it!*

I knew it was Valimus in my head, but I did not care. I even saw his reflection in the glass, where mine should have been. His toothy grin mocked me. I did not care. All of the blood, violence, and hunting changed me. It morphed me into the monster that I knew I was becoming.

The window slid open without making a noise. The smell of lavender from a can and freshly folded laundry assaulted my keen nostrils giving me a heady sensation. It was disorienting when contrasted with the grime, trash, and sooty smell of the urban jungle that was Culver's Bay. The edges of my mouth curled upward. My fangs stabbed into my mouth. The taste of worn pennies filled my mouth and spilled along the inside of my body. It hummed with a power no normal person could fathom.

Creeping inside I watched as my prey moved around unawares, cooking dinner and listening while a news program filled the room with its mindless, useless information.

"…and onto other news. The serial killer labeled 'The Tooth Fairy' has struck again, this time closer to home in Culver's Bay. There has been a recent rash of murders linked to the serial killer. Each murder has been different, but the one strange link is the missing teeth of each victim. This time his grisly victims were disemboweled, partially eaten and, in some cases, evidence suggests that the victims' corpses have been recently dug up from their graves. This is very similar to his first victim in Culver's Bay, one Michael Lubeski. This has been linked to multiple murders and slaughters that have occurred across the country for the past seven years. The most horrific case being in New Orleans where The Tooth Fairy ransacked an abandoned plantation occupied by a several young runaways. They were each shot, burned, and had their teeth extracted…"

The newscaster continued recounting my violent incidents. My victim walked across the living room and stared at the screen. I watched from the darkened bedroom as my prey stared enraptured by the news story.

"The killer at large has been doggedly pursued by the FBI." The image of the anchor was replaced by footage of the parking structure where I fought the rogue vampire Valimus unleashed on me. In the foreground was a haggard-looking man wearing a suit. Beneath the man's face were the words: FBI Special Agent Jack Andrews. My body shivered. I never knew that there was someone following me from state to state, walking amid my carnage. I never know that even as a predator, I was also prey. After all the demons I have destroyed and all the buildings I have set aflame to cover my tracks, still someone is out there stalking me.

Even from several feet away and through a television screen, I could see the fire in his eyes. His heart was filled with a desire and fury that has driven him to seek me out. The zeal I have for hunting vampires was mirrored in his desire to see me arrested.

He is hunting you, Gabriel. Valimus' words rang in my head. *He will get you. As sure as I have gotten you, he will seek you, find you, and capture you. You will be placed in a cell where you will live out a miserable existence until your end. Then ... you will become one of us.*

My eyes flared red.

"...has eluded capture for the past seven years. He is bloodthirsty and vicious. He strikes quickly and violently, leaving no witnesses."

"What do you know about this ... Tooth Fairy?" an off-camera reporter asked. Rachel seemed enraptured in the news piece. Her body shivered, as if she was crying.

"He's Caucasian, roughly thirty to forty years of age and is very crafty about hiding his insanity. Most likely he is delusional; he hides his ulterior motives under an alter ego facade."

"Alter ego? As in..." the journalist chuckled, "...a ... superhero type of fashion?"

"Precisely. He thinks he is doing the world a favor. Most likely a pseudo-vigilante type of mindset. However, what he is doing is killing innocent people under the perception that he is doing good."

The world shuddered all around me. This creature was twisting what I was doing into a perverted mockery.

We can get anyone, Valimus whispered in my head. *Humans are not outside our reach.*

The cop was wrong. I did not see myself as a hero. It is true that at one point I did. I saw what I did as righting wrongs. That was when I thought the Voices were instructions from God. That was before I thought what I did was not murder, that to kill something that was already dead was different than taking a life. Killing was killing, no matter what the creature. I knew this now and I knew that I was a monster. Perhaps I was just as bad as the demons that I hunted. Valimus did what he did with a perverted ideology that he was advancing the evolutionary process. He believed he was enriching the species. What was I doing? Was I killing for the sake of it? Did I enjoy what I did?

I refused to let the line of questioning in my mind go any further. That was when I gripped one of the cross-shaped daggers in my pocket. The glinting sheen of the blade gleamed in the dimmed room. The bloodlust grew inside of me, something that was as easy to do as breathing lately. I let the demon inside of me have free reign.

Her back was to me. She continued to cry. *Why was she crying?* I shrugged off the concern. I could not think about that. I could kill her without her knowing what happened. She had seen me walking from the slaughterhouse that was my motel room. That was unacceptable. She needed to die.

And I could slake my thirst.

I had fallen off the wagon. There was no need to pretend. I was what I was.

A vampire. A predator.

It had served me well and it would do so again … tonight.

Moving soundlessly into the room, I came ever closer to my prey.

Rachel.

I bared my fangs. They glistened wet with saliva and need.

Just a sip.

I can stop whenever I want to.

I merely *choose* not to.

"Among the victims is one Richard Matheson Stoker." The newscaster left me dumbstruck. "He has been missing for the past seven years. The FBI has presumed him dead, victim to the Tooth Fairy's carnage; however, no body has been found." I stared at the screen. Rachel turned around and I dove behind a nearby couch to stay hidden from my prey.

You have him, don't you? I thought knowing Valimus would hear me.

What do you mean? Of course, I don't have him. His voice was thick with humor.

He is the key to all of this, isn't he? He was your first!

You have no idea what you're talking about. He is dead. Just leave him be.

The fear in his words excited me. I knew I was getting close.

My thoughts were interrupted when I heard Rachel coming closer. I tensed from my position on the floor. *She wouldn't look down,* I thought. I could trip her and before she knew what was happening. I could open her throat. I could drink the hot salty fluids. It would only take a few seconds.

It was that easy.

Death is easy; living is the hard part.

Just as I was going to enact my fantasy, there was a knock on her door. The footsteps receded and I slipped back into my previous position in her bedroom. I watched from the shadows as she opened the door and let Dr. Jack Worth into her home.

"I came as soon as I could. What is the urgency?" His face held nothing but concern and confusion.

"It came true again." Her body shook. The good doctor held her in his arms, consoling her.

"It's okay," he lied. "Everything's going to be alright. Just tell me what happened."

"It's like I told you. I dreamt it. I went to the motel and watched as … as … *he* came out of the room. He was like a monster. He was a living breathing shadow and he ran to a car and drove away. Then, I … I…" She paused and took another deep breath. "I walked to the room and saw … them."

"The bodies?" Worth asked. He stroked her shoulders. She nodded. "Were they…?"

"I know it was all a dream, but it just-just…" The doctor led her to the couch and they sat down. I grabbed the Beretta. I had to kill them, especially if she revealed my name to him. She was an innocent. The doctor was in this up to his eyeballs, but I couldn't prove it. It was gut feeling. A cool, calculating part of me did not want to kill him. I knew he could lead me to Valimus and reveal his connection in all of this. But if she told him…

I sighted along the barrel of the gun and lined the blade between the eyes of the alcoholic woman.

"What happened in your dream?" His voice was soothing and she bought into it, hook, line, and sinker.

So she talked. She regaled him with everything that had happened in her dream. I listened to her talk of a monster in a motel room with several mangled bodies. She talked of how he defiled them and tore them to shreds with a wicked knife. She mentioned how he held a corpse and cut its intestines out while its innards spilled all over him. It seemed like déjà vu. Rachel was describing the incident at the motel, but she was wrong. She had it all wrong. Was she psychic? Did she "see" a distortion of the true events in that motel room? Was she a minion of Valimus'? Did she tell Worth this because she wanted to paint me out to be a psychopath? A part of me felt so betrayed. She was my confidant. She wasn't supposed to lie to me…or about me. She nodded. "I don't want to see this anymore." Tears ran down her eyes. "I am tired of … *seeing*."

"How is the medication working? Are you able to sleep at night now?"

"Yes, but they still come! The dreams…they're still there! He kills and kills and then … their … *teeth*…" The gun shivered in my hand. My finger tightened on the trigger.

Kill her! Valimus screamed! *Kill her! She knows too much!*

My finger tensed on the trigger. *She's lying!* I thought, outraged.

"*God, grant me the Serenity to accept the things I cannot change, the Courage to change the things I can, and the Wisdom to know the difference.*"

I made the sign of the cross as I preyed (or was it "prayed"?).

****

What is it with a man's character that makes him a man? What is it that makes him monster? Where do we draw the line?

I wondered this as I placed the crosshairs of my gun, a gun that I took off of a dead man nearly seven years ago, on the beautiful profile of Rachel. She was a woman I once thought of as innocent, but now I have my doubts.

The weapon was heavy with my need. I listened to those lies that she spewed and I wanted to kill her for it. She needed to be silenced. Beads of sweat obscured my vision. They fell down my face. I blinked back the salty streams and wiped my forearm across them, trying to keep my focus. It was difficult, so I took a double-handed stance on the weapon. I could end them both with a few pulls from my weapon. *Do it!* I wasn't sure if that was my mind or Valimus. Everything began to blur together.

My focus drifted. Maybe it was the lack of sleep or the screams that I keep hearing, but I found it hard to steady my aim. My mind wandered. A cross hung on the wall next to me. It was a simple symbol, but it was a powerful one. My mind fled back to that moment (mere hours ago), when I wrestled with that ravenous vampire and I felt the burn of his cross on my cheek. God gave me a reprieve from Hell, even if it was for a few hours or days. Why did He do such a thing?

He didn't do it just so I could kill a woman who had only a peripheral part to play in this whole sordid fiasco. This weapon has solved a lot of my problems over the years. I do not use the gun as a tool to help others. This weapon is a problem-solver for me. Rather than being rational, my first instinct is to eliminate my problems. Is this what makes me a monster? Why, God, did you spare me? *The Lord works in mysterious ways.* That's a damned understatement.

Slowly, I lowered the Beretta. She did not need to die just to serve some sick twisted logic that Valimus was concocting in my cerebral cortex.

"You won't win this day, Valimus," I whispered. "I may not have much of a soul, but what little of it I have you won't get that easily." I continued to listen to their conversation.

Afterwards, I stood at the bottom of the fire escape that I used. I thumbed through my copy of Alcoholics Anonymous. I knew my defects, and they were many, but was I ready to ask God to help me remove them?

Even if I was ready, the bigger question is: Would God even want to help me?

Step Seven

"Humbly asked Him to remove our shortcomings"

"Mom, could you please do it? Please?" The boy pulled the heavy blankets up to his chin and looked wild-eyed at his mother. "I won't ask you again." His lie was blatant.

Jessica Winthrop sat on the edge of her son's bed. "Ryan, you are getting too big for this."

"Please, Mommy?" He said it in that voice that all children learn; the voice that cuts to the quick of people with mercy and makes them do their bidding.

"Okay. Okay." Her sigh was indignant.

The woman stood up and strode to the closet located to the far right of the bed. She opened the door wide enough for him to eye it from over the thickness of his blanket. "Do you see? There are no monsters in the closet. It's all imagined. All in your head."

Ryan Winthrop nodded, but did not look relaxed by this revelation in the slightest. He knew the truth.

There *are* monsters in the darkness.

I stood on the roof of the two-storied brownstone and looked inside the boy's bedroom. It was decorated as every boy's room across the country should be: cars, action figures, Nerf basketball hoop above the door. He was the picture of normalcy.

Did he know that within his beating heart, a monster lay dormant?

Do *any* of us know this?

****

When you are an addict, it is so easy to slip back into the cycle of addiction. *One sip will take the edge off. Really, what is the harm in one tiny sip?* It allows you to get through the tough times. *Tomorrow, I'm done.*

It was lies; all of it. And I *knew* it.

So why was it so damned hard to lower the gun? I wondered this just two hours ago while I was peeking in on another target.

The Beretta trembled in my grip. Even though it weighed ten tons, I continued to keep my two-handed stance in the shadows of the enigmatic "Rachel" and the dirty Dr. Jack Worth.

"I want to see you at my office. We can run some tests-"

"I won't be your guinea pig!" The beautiful woman's outburst jolted me. I gasped, hoping the weapon wouldn't fire. She shot up from the couch and walked to a bookcase where she sat her cigarettes and lighter. It was only after she had taken six puffs on the cancer stick before her racing pulse slowed. My skin crawled at the thought of so much carbon monoxide mingling in with her lungs.

Damned smokers! Valimus spat in my mind. *They make the blood taste weak. Tainted!* He echoed my thoughts.

"I-I'm sorry." The goth girl ashed on her carpet. She wore a t-shirt displaying some metal band and ripped faded jeans. Her bare arms displayed tattoos that told a tragic story. They were the visual art of a tortured soul. "I've ... I've been there, man."

"I am not pretending that Amhearst was a picnic ... for you or anybody. You did what you were supposed to do and you came out a better person for it."

Rachel? Sh-she was in Amhearst? What did they do to her? My trigger finger rested on the guard, but I slid it back along the trigger itself. Was she like me?

There it was. The connection that I felt with her had a reason. It was why I wanted to kill her. She was just like … Claire DeWalt. The world grew cloudy. Was Valimus controlling more than my cravings? Was he controlling my senses, too?

The fluid that slid from my eyes told me he had nothing to do with it. It was *her*. DeWalt ran a bed and breakfast in a secluded little town that I went to in order to investigate a string of murders that had a vampire's MO. She was nice to me. She made me feel as if I could be normal.

And I killed her for it.

Claire was a homicidal blend of human and monster wrapped up in a Martha Stewart package. Even though I am ninety percent sure that Martha Stewart was a demon, Clair fooled me into thinking she was innocent. The pie-baking succubus was torturing an elderly vampire couple for blood, which she spiked with cocaine to give her a boost during daylight hours. She had me addicted to the vamp smack for awhile.

So I killed her and tore the fangs from the witch's head!

But she got deep inside of me. Like a parasite, she latched onto me and fed from my soul.

Just like this demon was doing.

Once again, I aimed the Beretta right at her skull. My finger wrapped around the trigger, ready to squeeze like a sadistic boa constrictor.

"It didn't matter what you or that damned Dr. Winthrop put me on. The dreams still come. They still have that shadowy monster that hunted, killed and bled hundreds of people." She paced the room, a caged leopardess anxious to be let loose.

A plan formed in my head.

No! Valimus raged.

My smile was icy. I faded into the deep shadows of the bedroom.

****

The crack of thunder lashed across the back of nightfall; the white colored wound of lightning bled across a nightmarish cityscape. Tears from heaven fell over dark reality while I observed my prey from the fire escape of Rachel's apartment building. The alley that I spied my quarry from overlooked the parking lot where my prey had parked his foreign sedan. Rain drooled from the barrel of my gun. My desire to shed blood was overwhelming.

Sharp fangs stabbed into my gums from behind sealed lips. The sneer I wore was more from pain than the plan that formed from my dark thoughts.

Kill him, Valimus whispered. Desperation coated each syllable.

That's what you want, I responded. *You want their secrets to die with them. They hold the key to fulfilling your sadistic prophecy.*

Yes, he replied, *but which one? Is it the woman with the otherworldly thoughts? The one who has seen you kill in her very dreams? Could it be the doctor with the secrets? Is it his insidious mind that holds the key to your mystery? Do not forget the little boy who is the spawn of one of our own.*

His mocking tone gestated inside my guts, growing larger and consuming me from the inside. His thoughts were alive and feeding my addiction.

There is one way to end it all.

He was right. There was one way to make sure his prophecy would not come to fruition.

That was to kill them all.

Could I do it? Could I kill a child? Did I have it in me to kill an innocent woman whose only crime was to dream? Was I the monster I thought myself to be?

Once my victim took to the streets in his car, I gave chase in my pilfered vehicle. The rain attacked my car. The barrage of water was a hail of bullets striking the roof and hood. A biting chill filled the car, but I had the air conditioner on full blast. The cold fed the demon inside of me, supercharging my preternatural side which gave me amassed strength.

The luxury sedan wound through the labyrinthine net-work of back alleys informally called The Ways. Streets named Broadway, Crestway, Hillway, and others were narrow passages filled with discarded trash and discarded people. Empty eyes flashed at us as we passed. At times, when it was just my car and the good doctor's on the road, I turned the headlights off and navigated by my vampiric night vision. I knew where we were going, but I kept his car in sight anyway.

****

The crackle of thunder and flash of lightning created a macabre mood once I turned the engine off and was plunged into the all too comfortable darkness. Jack parked his car in the driveway of Dr. and Mrs. Winthrop and jogged to the front of the house. Looking down at the wet 9mm weapon, I knew I was a monster. The easiest scenario for me would be to kill every liv-ing and *un*living being in that house. It would put a halt to Valimus' evil scheme.

So many people had died up to this point. So many peo-ple screamed their last cries at me before I ended their existence. Every single one of them *looked* to be human.

But they weren't!

Right?

I looked upwards into the midnight sky; the angry weather exploded into a bright, white flash. *God, what kind of monster am I?* I asked. I wanted to beg Him for help, to ask Him to change me for the better. Another crackle of thunder an-swered my unasked question.

Earlier this evening, Miranda Baltimore had told me that Valimus had concocted this whole evil "Council" scheme to play some twisted mind game with me. I had always thought they were organized and living in shadow to bide their time before … before what?

If they weren't organized, then what were they? Was it as simple as wild beasts roaming the cities and countries feeding on an unholy addiction? If so, then who was "Dr. Winthrop" working for? What does that say about Valimus' whole "prophecy" thing?

And most importantly, what did that say about my memories of being in Facility, the multiple voices in my head, and my sanity?

How do I fight all of that?

Before I could think of a possible answer, the doctor left the house and hopped into his car. While he drove away, I checked the digital clock.

An hour had passed.

The silhouette of Jessica Winthrop appeared in the bay window of the two-story brownstone. My car was parked across the street from the Winthrop residence. Mrs. Winthrop's position at the window gave her a clear view of my car.

She could see me. I knew it.

I just didn't give a damn.

Valimus whispered dark thoughts in my mind, and they made a lot of sense. His twisted logic shaped a reality that was better for all of us. It was a world where I wanted to live.

It would be a better place for us all.

With darkness in my heart and benevolence infecting my soul, I gripped the wet steel and opened the car door…

****

I spent another hour on the roof of the Winthrop residence. I stood outside of my prey's bedroom, my finger slid along the cool edge of a dagger. A flash of lightening and he saw me.

"Mommy! Mom!" I inched away from the pane of glass. My heart nearly exploded from my chest.

"Th-th-there's a monster outside my window." His voice was breathless.

I heard Jessica burst into her son's room.

"Out there! He's out there!"

"There's nothing out there, sweetie." The beautiful wife of Malfric stood mere feet away from my position. Her voice was louder. She had to be right next to the window. "It's raining cats and dogs out there. There is no way anything would be lurking outside."

"W-w-well, what about the closet?"

"There are no monsters in your closet, Ryan. I am not going to check. You are too big of a boy for this." Irritation was thick in her voice.

"Mom, could you please do it? Please?"

Only when I was sure that they weren't looking at the window, did I risk spying on them again.

It's all imagined, she'd told her son before she left to go downstairs. *All in your head.* Some things are waiting in your closet. Some monsters are real.

The woman turned off her son's lamp and headed down the stairs. That was when I leapt from the ledge of the room.

By the time both feet touched wet pavement, the world exploded in a quick flash of light. I was standing right in front of the picture window as Jessica Winthrop gazed outside. In that instant lighting, Jessica's eyes met mine. She took in the black sweater, black slacks, midnight overcoat, and dead face, and drowned in fear. My tongue slid across her panic; it tasted like ripe lemons, tart but oh so tasty. My fangs slid into position and the world was as bright as day, even in this dead of night.

The panic was stark naked behind her eyes. She disappeared from sight, most likely heading upstairs to protect her son.

My target.

The prediction that Valimus spoke of had to be contained within this child. Every fiber of my being pulsed with this fact. There was no question of that in my mind anymore. Everything seemed to make so much sense.

Instead of breaking the front door down, I jogged around to the garage and broke into the room by kicking open the side door. With a gleaming silver dagger, I slashed the tires before heading into the backyard. Using my enhanced sight, I located the wire for the phone line and yanked it out.

Then, I destroyed the circuit box. Sparks sprayed the yard as the house went black.

My addiction was not merely to the taste of blood. If someone were to supply me with packets of warm O positive or AB negative, I would be flying high, but only for so long. Sooner or later, I would be craving the hunt. It wasn't just the blood that I needed.

It was the thrill of the hunt and the anticipation of the kill.

I smashed the patio window that led into the kitchen and breakfast nook of the large home. My pulse throbbed in my ears. I tried to focus past Valimus' laughter only to realize that my tormentor was not laughing. The true horror was the realization that the insidious chuckling came from me!

Lifting my nose to the room, I opened myself up to smells that no normal person could pick up. The spices of the kitchen cabinets assaulted my nostrils. Each of them competed for my attention. Yesterday's laundry scents still hung in the air.

Ten paces into the living room and I caught it. That sickly sweet aroma that was slight, but unmistakable.

The odor of panic.

The faint throbbing of two pulsing heartbeats echoed in my skull. The pulsations created a primal song pounded out by ancient drums. It sang an epic of hunters emerging from fire-lit caves. Savages grunting monosyllabic orders to enter a wooded fray, searching for food.

For blood … *fresh* blood!

Another crackle of lightning and an almost inaudible gasp of fright drew my attention. I slid the gun into my deep pocket and palmed a dagger. Another shock of lightning reflected off the steel. Guns were so clean. They were too easy. My maw drooled with anticipation.

The soft cry came from upstairs. My wet, heavy boots creaked as they fell atop each step.

They knew I was coming.

Good, I thought. It'll make the blood taste all the sweeter. Fear pumps the blood faster through the body. It accentuates the salty taste, mingling with a coppery aftertaste.

"I-i-is he ... gone, Mommy?"

To those of us that are sensitive to the preternatural, we know that air acts in the same way as water. If you throw a pebble into a lake the waters are disturbed and a ripple effect occurs. Sound disturbs the air in the same way. Those "disturbances" spurred me onward. I climbed those stairs with murder in my heart. The Darkness eclipsed me, filling me with that same unnatural coldness that has been with me every time I stalk one of *them*.

Once I stood on the upstairs landing, I faced the long hallway. *The child is the key*, I thought. *His death will end this whole nightmare.* Oddly, standing on the landing of that hallway as the world lit up in a black and white hell, I felt a sense of déjà vu. I was doing this before. The fear of a child, the screams of a woman, a darkened house ... all of it felt familiar. *I was here before, I was here before, I was here before.* My brain repeated the same thing again and again.

I entered the empty room. The air was not disturbed; all was still. Never making a sound, I moved to the next room, a bathroom, which was also empty. In my mind's eye, I was holding a shotgun. Why? Why did all of this seem so familiar? Why the shotgun?

I found the two of them in a corner of the large walk-in closet in the master bedroom. Jessica Winthrop, who looked every bit as beautiful as the picture I found in Malfric's wallet before I buried him alive in the Nevada desert, held onto her son, protecting him from the monster that stood silhouetted in the doorway.

"Please, n-not my son," she whimpered.

In our AA meetings, the addicts that shared all told of The Moment. In each of their experiences, there was a moment that they clearly remember having to choose. Did they take that drink? Did they put it back on the bar and walk out?

This was my Moment.

It would be so easy to walk in and tear them to shreds with silver and fangs. Images of rending flesh and thick, steamy, salty blood awashed my body in waves of ecstasy. My body shivered.

Valimus' laugh boomed behind my eyes. He even forced my hand to raise the dagger in my tight grip.

"Just let my son go." Tears streamed from her pleading eyes.

"When the indigo aura turns midnight, the apocalypse begins."

"Your son is the key to this ... to all of this." I took a step into the closet. "Do you think I *want* to do this? Contrary to what you may think, I am not a monster." I raised the blade even higher. "I am not a monster!"

Then, another boom of thunder and flash of lighting...

My body grew weaker. I could barely keep the blade in my hand. What I had thought to be the weather was actually a gunshot.

Slowly, I turned to look behind me. I found that same man from the news telecast that I saw in Rachel's apartment, standing in the bedroom. His eyes held a grimness that I have only seen in my undead prey. Agent Jack Andrews' weapon never wavered from me, but I knew I was faster. I never knew what it was like to be stalked. He has followed me across the country just like I have my undead prey.

"Drop your weapon and come out with your hands up!"

I stood on rubbery legs looking at the scared little boy. His cheeks were wet; his eyes were wide. He was drenched in fear so succulent, that the mere smell made me want to risk certain doom and damnation.

I made my decision just as the weather opened up with a vicious onslaught. With the fierceness of a demon from the bowels of Hell, I leapt at the man with the gun.

I bowled him over just has he fired another shot from his weapon. The bullet scored a trail along my right shoulder. With a ferocious roar, I clamped my fangs over his shoulder, near the collarbone. My efforts were rewarded with a scream from the agent.

"Go! Go!" he screamed at my intended prey.

By the time I looked up from my victim, the Winthrop's were headed out of the bedroom. Jessica looked back and screamed. My mouth dripping black blood, a serpentine hiss slid from my lips.

Unfortunately, the quick distraction gave Agent Andrews enough time to sucker punch me in the jaw. The blow knocked me off the prone cop. Reality pin-wheeled and I dove into the closet just as more thunderous explosions lit up the night. The agent's aim was sloppy. Was it because of the wound, or the shocked look on his face? "I know you! You-you look … familiar. Who are you?" I didn't relish the idea of trading shots with a federal agent, but I hated the thought of bleeding to death in a dark closet even worse.

I could see his mind calculating. He decided to take a more desperate tactic. "I've got you dead to rights, you bastard!" His voice was touched with hysteria. The fresh blood pumping from my bullet wound drove my senses wild. Worst of all, for the fed, it made me ravenous. "Surrender and toss out your gun. I promise that I'll have the wound treated." I could hear his ragged breathing as he checked his wound. "Otherwise, I have no problem letting you die in there."

"What makes you think that you aren't going to be the one to die?" I asked in a low voice. I am sure Andrews never heard me, but Valimus did.

And he laughed.

I stood in the darkness of the closet, hunkered down and ready to strike. Blood drizzled from my body just as the rain did from the obsidian sky. The monster in Ryan Winthrop's closet, the beast that he knew lurked in the shadows every night before he went to bed, took corporeal form and was cornered by a man who was trying to do what was right.

"You don't know how long I've been waiting for this, Tooth Fairy." The man's voice tinged with dementia. It was a timbre I knew all too well. "You're not getting away from me, you bastard. Not again." It forced a smile from Valimus' soul, which appeared on my face. A part of me knew at that moment that the demon in my head was a part of me. Valimus did not merely take a peek in my mind every now and then. He was a part of my mind, my psyche. Under normal circumstances, this would have frightened me to ponder the ramifications of this, but in my situation, I had little time to think about that. One thing was certain...

It made me a lot more dangerous than I thought that I was.

A small part of me wondered why he was so intent on capturing me. The crackle in his voice suggested that there was something else to his motives. Something more personal.

I moved to the edge of the shadows and watched the agent's fear swirl in the air around him. It fueled my addiction, making me long for the scent of blood ... his blood. Using more reserves of the ebbing strength that I did have, I worked on pushing the monster to the corners of my mind. "My addiction is my weakness," I whispered to myself. "My addiction is my weakness." I pressed my hands together, intertwining the fingers. "God, please help me." I could not remember parts of my life before all of this, but I am getting to know the person that I am. I know that I am a proud man and not very humble. It is hard to ask for help. To this day I credit myself with that step towards healing, asking for help. I knew that I had a problem, but it was up to me to ask for help. Perhaps, there was hope for me yet.

The federal agent's grip on his handgun shivered; my eyes gleamed with anticipation. He was faltering, weakening. My hope for control was slipping as my desire for murder grew. Agent Andrews shuffled closer to the closet. The time was drawing near. Confrontation was inevitable. One of us would not be able to walk out of this the same. I didn't want to kill him, but...

That moment before we struck, I thought of Jessica Winthrop sitting at her son's bedside, doing what every mother is supposed to do: lie to her son that there was no such thing as monsters, and convince their child that there were no monsters in their closets.

Yes, Mrs. Winthrop, there *are* monsters in the closet, and you would be coming face to face with one very soon.

Step Eight

"Made a list of all persons we had harmed and became willing to make amends to them all."

Agent Jack Andrews was an adult, but as he looked into the mouth of the dark closet, he was peering through the eyes of a frightened little boy. One hand clutched his wounded shoulder, trying to stem the tide of blood that flowed from his delicious wound. The other held, in a shaky grip, a Beretta 9mm, similar to the one I held in my hand.

The demon in my head whispered again. *He cannot see into the darkness. You have a clear shot!*

"Stop it!" I yelled. I forced myself to place my stolen Beretta in the waistband of my pants.

"Stop what?" The confusion on the federal agent's face was pain to see.

He is getting in your way. Your prey is escaping.

The demon in my head was playing a game and I was falling into it. He was right. They were getting away. The family of the vampire that had tortured me for years in The Facility was running into the night, thanks to this fed. I needed to get the child. Ryan Winthrop was part of the prophecy; Valimus needed Ryan to fulfill his sick plans. However, he wanted me to do the dirty work. Valimus wanted me to descend into the depths of madness. *You must kill him! He is intent on killing you. There is nothing in this man that wants to let you live.*

"I … won't … kill … him." My teeth were clenched. Sweat poured from my face and drenched my sweater. Once I focused on my breathing, I was able to push away the seductive call of the fed's bloody wound.

You don't have much time left. You're bleeding to death. Then, you will become one of us. No longer will you be able to sit on the sidelines. The Call will be too strong for you to ignore. You will become … me!

"No!" I roared.

The agent shivered. "K-kick the gun out to me. I promise you will be unharmed."

Lies! Valimus screamed. The federal agent's fear caused my monster, my addiction, to gain strength. The need overwhelmed me, pushing all reason away. I shoved the weapon into my pocket. The deep addiction in my soul yearned to tear away pieces of him.

The small part of me that was still human prayed for the agent. I was powerless to stop the thirst. There was nothing I could do. Perhaps there was something God could do. Yes, I was damned, but the agent was not.

"Dear God, please save him!" I screamed as I charged forward.

The flash of light from the muzzle of his gun was blinding, but I charged anyway. Somehow, the monster in me weakened, allowing humanity to dominate. Our bodies collided; the force of the blow propelled Andrews across the room, while I continued. I couldn't stop even if I wanted to.

My body exploded through the plate glass window of the bedroom. Razor shards of glass sliced me to ribbons; the pain reminded me of what a stupid decision I'd made. The bullet wound Andrew left in me burned while I twisted my body, falling through midnight. As bad as that was, it wasn't the worst part. The worst part was the landing. Every bone in my body rattled upon impact. My wounds screamed, my vision blurred, and the taste of a million pennies filled my mouth.

Surely, I was dying.

You're not dead, yet, Valimus taunted. *You're not that lucky.*

Getting to my feet proved to be more difficult than I thought. I wasted precious moments stumbling around. Once I got my legs under me, I jogged into the darkness.

****

"The earliest memory I have is a scream in the darkness."

"Can you describe this scream?" he asked in that calm voice they always use.

"What do you mean?" I asked. "How do you describe a … scream?" Perhaps he'd hypnotized me. Perhaps he made me think that he was normal, a human.

"Was it your scream? Was it urgent? I mean … a scream of fear or of pain?"

"A scream is always urgent." I shifted in the leather chair. It creaked. Looking around the office, I could tell he wanted to project masculinity, power, and authority. Degrees and awards adorned the wall behind him. The fake wood paneling was dark. The desk that sat between us was marble; it looked heavy. "It was a woman's voice. She was afraid."

"What is she afraid of?" He steepled his fingertips. They brushed the underside of his nose while he squinted his eyes, which scrutinized me with the cold, merciless calculations of a serpent. Speed, agility, accuracy: the attributes of a predator.

"Was."

"Excuse me?" The word caught him off guard.

So I repeated it. "*Was*. What *was* she afraid of?" I followed it up with those dreaded three words. "She is dead."

****

I never sat with any of the others. I knew they had *it*. I wasn't as infected as they were and I wanted to keep it that way.

The tray of food always looked innocent enough, but I knew it contained sedatives and mind-altering chemicals designed to weaken my resolve. They were smart. They existed for centuries without our knowledge. They even created fictional literature and films for us to digest so we could not know the difference between reality and illusion.

Scanning the sea of faces across the lunch room, I knew that only a few of us would live past the end of the week. Their screams echoed in my mind as the vampire guards escorted me back to my padded cell every single day.

I always sat next to the barred window with the wire mesh zig-zagging over the pane. It looked out over the courtyard where we were allowed to walk. Vampire/human hybrids that weren't killed by sun would bring us back inside. I watched them prod the living with nightsticks to make sure the humans were corralled and brought inside. As I stared through the window, the eyes of Valimus reflected back at me. He stood in the image and grinned that sadistic smile.

They are turning us into them. His voice had the lunacy of a religious zealot.

"You mean vampires?"

No! The one word held enough power to chill my insides. *I mean puppets for them. We are evolving into what we were supposed to become, but they will not use us to our full potential. We will simply be sheep. That is all they will want us to be.* I watched him staring back at me. His lips never moved, but his voice was plain as day in my mind. *It is telepathy,* he explained. *We are bound by blood. We all are.*

The large hand of one of the guards clamped over my shoulder. I looked up at the large man who looked back at me with obsidian eyes. He smiled a sharp-toothed grin.

"What am I?" I pleaded as the guard pulled me from my chair. When I returned my gaze to the window, I saw the face of my enemy mocking me. He wore the same smile as the guard.

Us, they both answered in my mind.

****

Before I opened my eyes, I heard that woman's scream again. Her fear wrapped around me in the darkness; my body shuddered while I attempted to pry my eyelids open.

"He's coming to." The voice was so far away.

"Be careful. You don't know anything about him. Look at him! He looks like he's been through a damned war." This second voice held wisdom in its pitch.

The first thing I saw once my eyes could focus was an intricate grid of heavy pipes. Just behind them were grimy bricks. I wretched at the putrid smell that invaded my nose and mouth. My stomach worked to push its contents out, but I had not eaten in some time.

Slowly, the dirty, worn face of a young woman slid into view. She pressed a cold, wet cloth onto my forehead. The hammer-like pounding that smashed against the inside of my skull receded.

"Get away from him, Arlene." The urgent voice was a male's. "He's dangerous. Did you see what Caleb pulled from his jacket? Looks like an assassin to me."

"Doesn't seem like an assassin. Just lay off the conspiracy theories, Alfonso." Another masculine voice was nearby.

"What the hell does an assassin 'seem' like?" The voice belonging to "Alfonso" raised an octave. It trembled with a slight onset of paranoia and insanity. However, the guy did have a point.

"Tim. Alfonso. Be quiet." That wise voice returned. As the young woman's face gained more focus, another face came into view. This one was of a man with leathery skin. His head was haloed in snow white, as was the lower portion of his face. Once my eyes blinked out the haziness, I noticed him scrutinize me with electric blue eyes. They were kind eyes; the eyes a man would give his grandchild each time he visited.

The wise man gave a warm smile. "My name is Caleb." He looked over at the younger woman who stood next to him.

"This shy, little thing is Arlene." After a pause, he asked, "Can you tell us your name?"

It took me several tries, but I managed to croak, "Gabe." The old man smiled, reminding me of a college professor named Rex Stillwater, a man I have never met.

"You have lost a lot of blood." Caleb kept the smile, but it dimmed along its edges. I turned my head. A rickety makeshift rack that held a bag of oh so delicious fluid stood to my right. An IV that tapped into the vein on my right arm served as the soothing of warmth, feeding my addiction. I could feel my power returning.

Little did they know that it may very well have meant their own undoing.

"I was able to extract the glass from your wounds. The … the wound…" I knew he was trying to refer to the bullet that grazed me. "…uh … that was superficial." He paused, and looked towards the tall black man with the unkempt braids who stood in the corner of the burnt-out room we were in. He fingered a length of pipe and mumbled something about guarding the perimeter. The steel slapped against the leather of his fingerless gloves. "Alfonso" stared at me with thinly veiled suspicion.

I returned my gaze to Caleb. "Don't worry. You have nothing to fear from me." Lies slid from my lips so effortlessly. I have always wondered if I could lie so well because I did not have a soul.

"Oh yeah?" The black man stepped forward. From his waistband, he grabbed the Beretta, my Beretta, and aimed it at me. "Then why do you have this?"

Why, indeed, Valimus taunted.

For a moment, I wondered if the paranoid man would shoot me. He would have been better off if he had.

"Easy, Al," the other man, "Tim", said. He was short and stocky. A wool cap covered the top of his head. His jaw line was shaggy, but severely angled, reminding me of pulp drawings in comic books. He eyed me curiously. The man stepped towards me and cocked his head to one side. I felt like a monarch butterfly pinned to a corkboard.

I was just as helpless.

"Alfonso has served our country faithfully," Caleb said by way of explanation. "However, he has witnessed some dark events in his servitude."

"You don't need to speak for me!" His head moved erratically, causing the thick, black tendrils to whip across his face. He forced himself to lower the weapon. I'm sure the man knew he looked crazy.

"I am sorry, Al, but you are scaring our patient." Caleb turned to me and tried to calm me with a hand atop my shoulder. Strangely enough, it worked.

"Why did you help me?" My voice cracked.

"That's a damned good question." Alfonso looked at Caleb. "He looks like shit and obviously trouble."

"H-h-how did you look when you showed up here?" The meek girl's words echoed off the empty walls of the burned-out structure. Caleb smiled.

"She has a fine point." The patriarch stole a glance at the veteran, who looked away.

The rays of the approaching dawn sapped all energy from my battered body, submerging me beneath the waters of consciousness.

****

The nights brought me from my deep slumber. Each time the sun set, I would awaken with even more strength than before. It took me three full days to recover from the blood loss.

I consider myself lucky Caleb was a doctor in a former life. He told me that he still had contacts in the local hospital, where he worked. Some of the people in the streets have lost all trust in civilization, but they still need help, as the old man explained to me.

Thank God for men like him. I wonder about him. Is he in the caverns of Culver's Bay, working as a savior to the disenfranchised? Each evening I was introduced to "Dark City," a labyrinthine maze in downtown Culver's Bay where the refuse of society resided. It was a city within a city, an invisible reality that the citizenry refused to acknowledge.

It was the perfect place for me to be. Unfortunately, it was also the ideal for Valimus and the demons of the night to prey.

Trashcan fires painted tall, eerie phantasms along the towering walls of high rises which added to the claustrophobic atmosphere. Once again, Caleb led me through the "city." I wore a faded pair of blue jeans, a ratty, but warm, wool sweater, and a heavy skull cap in addition to my overcoat and work boots. Alfonso never returned my gun to me, but I still had my silver blades hidden along my coat. I did not feel safe with a paranoid psychotic in possession of a loaded weapon. Then again, I was most likely a more dangerous paranoid psychotic than *he* was.

The back alleys were littered with tents and other makeshift homes. The trashcan fires served as streetlights and street urchins ran through the "neighborhoods" singing songs that reminded me of a childhood I never had.

"Where do you come from?" Caleb tried to make the question seem innocent, and perhaps it was.

Hell, Valimus whispered from deep within my mind. The echoes of his taunting blended in with snapshot images of a life I had never lived. A life that jumped from a Norman Rockwell painting splashed across my mind's eye. I shuddered. Why was I seeing these images? Was I seeing through the eyes of Valimus, the devil that I knew? Or was it through the eyes of a demon I had yet to meet?

"Listen, Caleb, I appreciate everything that you have done for me, but-"

The sage waved off the comment. "The Hippocratic Oath … 'I will remember that I remain a member of society, with special obligations to all my fellow human beings, those sound of mind and body as well as the infirm.'" He paused as we walked past three older men warming their hands around an open fire.

One of them coughed a wet throaty sound. "That's Ed. He'll be gone ... in a few months."

"I know." My voice was granite. "I can smell it."

"I know you are a dangerous man; I knew that before we found the weapon on you. I also know you are a lost man, a confused man. Is there anything you can tell me-?"

"Why do you want to know?" The edge in my tone startled even me. I sighed, trying to be objective. "The longer I am here, the more of a danger you are in. There is a mission I must complete." I paused, and then added, "And I need to return to that mission."

The first thing I thought when I saw Caleb's expression was: fear. However, he did not reek of it. "There has been a lot of death on these streets as of late." His voice was a matter of fact tone. Perhaps Alfonso was wise to take my weapon.

"Oh?" I replied a little too eagerly.

"Someone is turning our city into a slaughterhouse." He paused, and then added, "Well, worse than it is already."

"Maybe it needs to be." We walked side by side in the cool, autumn night. The old man gazed into the urban darkness. Once we exited the claustrophobic maze of the towering buildings, the thunderous roar of the Culver's Bay's nearby river, nicknamed the Styx, he turned to me with shadows in his eyes.

"Gabriel, I have been a doctor for over thirty years. In those years in and out of residence, I have seen men who bring death. I know these men when I see them. Carnage and destruction accompany them. Some of them did it for ... noble reasons. Others did it for ... other reasons." His icy gaze forced me to avert my stare. That has never happened before. "I know you are a man who brings death. But I am not certain if you do it for noble reasons."

I do it for the most noble of reasons! I wanted to cry out. Unfortunately, I wasn't sure of that anymore. At one point, I was a single-minded zealot. I was sure of my righteous actions. Somewhere along the way, that black and white line had blurred into a shade of gray. Now, I was plotting to kill children and aiming a gun at an innocent girl. Somehow it turned from a crusade to a bloodbath. "I am not certain either." Looking over the rushing black waters, I reflected over the lives that I had taken ... as well as those I am about to take.

"Whether you do it for noble reasons or not does not concern me. Maybe it should." Out of the corner of my eye, I noticed he was staring at me. "You will bring death to my friends. I cannot allow that."

Caleb noticed my hand drifting to my jacket. He knew damn well I was going for one of the knives in my jacket. His face and body tensed. The man was waiting for death.

"What are you saying?" My voice was cold.

"I want you gone." His voice was frostier. "An eternity ago, I took that Hippocratic Oath. I may not be in the profession anymore, but I still uphold it. That was why I insisted on caring for you." He paused again. His eyes searched the midnight waters before us. I tried looking for that ferryman who would take me on my journey to Hades. "I cannot just let you endanger the lives of those I protect." He looked at my profile again. "Can you understand this?"

I could. I understood more than he would ever know.

"It is hard to turn my back on a fellow ... addict." His voice was a whisper.

Snapping my face to meet his nearly caused me whiplash. The smile on his face was warm, but sad. I was speechless, so he continued. "You haven't been in AA for long, have you?"

"No," I croaked.

Caleb reached into a pocket and produced a chip. "My five-year chip. That was given to me ten years ago." He gazed at it. "It's a reminder of where I came from and how easy pride can come before a fall." Caleb could see I wanted to know more but was too ashamed to ask. "They teach you how to save lives, but not how to cope with losing them." He laughed. "So I took to my friends: Jack Daniels and Jim Beam."

Caleb led me away from the dark waters where warehouses lined the streets. Dim streetlights cast deep shadows across the cityscape. As we walked, we dipped in and out of them. Caleb seemed at home in the darkness as much as I was. "It cost me everything. My family, my job, my life … all gone." His voice broke. "I broke that oath to do no harm when I lost a patient … while under the influence. A friend was on the review board. He gave me the option to resign, which I did. Before I knew it, I found myself here ... among other things."

"What else did you find?"

"Home, my dear boy. I found home."

We continued walking and he spoke of his journey to salvation and recovery. "I am in the process of making amends to those I have hurt and I have found that I have hurt many. My wife, my children…" He sighed. "I have not talked to them in years." He reached into his pocket and pulled out a weathered wallet. He opened the billfold and showed me an even more weathered photo. It was of a man who resembled Caleb, a beautiful woman and two children. "This was a man who had everything. A great practice, a beautiful family, and even a summer home. He lost it all to his battle with the bottle." He pointed to one of the two boys. "This is Alexander. He is getting his Master's degree in History. I found out he will be lined up to teach classes once he receives it. The other is Nicholas. He is a practicing lawyer in New York." He spoke like a proud parent. I wasn't sure how I knew what a proud parent felt like. For some reason it was a feeling that I knew. Before the Facility, did I have a family? My mind's eye flashed on the image of a child sleeping. His eyes opened, full of sleep. Then … a flash of lightning … and an overwhelming sadness.

Once again, I was back in reality, in the caverns of Dark City listening to Caleb and hearing his overwhelming sadness. "I am proud of them, but I know my life is worlds away from theirs.

I have seen them. I spied on them from afar and all of me wants to reach out to them, to touch them and tell them that I love them, but…" Another sigh. "Well, you know."

And I did know. I didn't think I was supposed to know, but somewhere, deep down, I understood. As we stood in the night of a burning trashcan, Caleb reached into his ratty, brown jacket pocket and produced a slender slip of paper. It was a list of names.

"This is a list of all the people that I have wronged." His smile was bittersweet. "It's a long list. I wasn't a nice man back in those days." He handed the list to me. "Someday, I want to confront each of these people and tell them just how sorry that I am."

"When do you want to do this?"

In response, the wise man smiled, "When I am less of a coward and am ready to face all of those people." Caleb's reply took me aback. To me, he was the bravest person in the world. He took care of people and places their needs above his own. It was evident that he was not afraid of loving someone, something that I saw as weakness, therefore was afraid of. "What will you do when you must face those that you have wronged?"

I thought about that seriously. "I don't know," I replied after a while. "I honestly don't know."

"Perhaps that is something that you should think about. It is part of the process."

"Process?" I looked at him.

"The healing process. You do want to get better, right?" He laughed. Of course, I want to get better … right?

****

As we walked through Dark City, the preternatural cold that always enveloped me grew in intensity. Icy tendrils of the undead part of me gripped my insides, frosting my lungs, heart, intestines, and other parts of my humanity. I pushed Caleb behind me and pressed both of us against the side of an apartment building.

"What is it?" the former physician asked.

"Ssshh," I hissed. Both of us stayed in the shadows and inched along the wall. Once we rounded a corner, red and blue flashes splashed against the harsh black brick, painting a portrait of fear … in both of us.

"The police!" Caleb gasped.

How did they find me? I wondered to myself.

"They roust us all the time. Every time there's a robbery some of them drive into Dark City and push us around." The wise man took the lead. "We must be quick. The last time they did this, we were beaten up badly. With Alfonso being as … agitated … as he was with you, there is no telling what he would do. He is a schizophrenic and has flashbacks whenever agitated."

"My gun!" My eyes grew wide. "He's got my gun!" The urgency spurred us along. We raced through the darkness as the flashes of emergency lights grew in intensity. The former doctor peered around a corner. I followed suit and watched as two men in blue uniforms proceeded to kick a citizen of Dark City who happened to be lying in the fetal position. Peering from a darkened corner and shielded by a trashcan, I noticed Arlene as she stared at the nightmarish tableau; her hands were clamped over her mouth. The shy girl's eyes were as wide as saucers. She shivered, but not from the autumn chill. *What is she doing there?* I wondered. My first instinct was to grab a silver dagger and storm into the fray, to kill the cops and drain them of every drop of blood.

However, the simple gesture of Caleb's hand on my elbow stopped me in my tracks. I spun around to face him, my eyes blazed with fury. I could feel the cold of the dead calling extra reserves of strength into my limbs. There was something in the sage's eyes that drained that supernatural strength, the strength that I was going to use to tear those men limb from limb. Caleb shook his head. The sadness in his eyes knew no bounds. As I started to walk away he retained his iron grip on my elbow.

"No," he said. "I want you to watch this."

"What?" I struggled to control my voice. "Wh-why?"

"I want you to know what it's like to see violence and *not* react to it."

I know the look in my eyes was of utter confusion. I knew he was speaking English because he used words like "you," "to," and "see," but other than that he was making no sense at all.

"Just … watch."

The police officers continued to use their batons to beat the helpless man who absorbed the blows. With each strike, the cold filled me with an icy fury. I trembled at the thought of spilling their blood. Little did Caleb know that he was forcing me to face my addiction. Looking at the act of brutality and injustice I felt something I had never felt before.

Helpless.

Just like my victims.

Arlene watched in silence and horror. Her small body trembled while tears streamed down her face. Her fear was raw, naked; it was unabashed and innocent. She was the reason I fought the "good fight." My soul was already damned; perhaps a part of me, the part that was still human, could spare the lives and innocence of people like her.

I was so enthralled by the pure beauty of the dirty, young woman that I failed to notice the movement in the darkness. It happened so quickly.

"Fucking pigs!" Alfonso's war cry shocked me back to reality. The shadows were shoved away as two muzzle flashes lit the night. Both police officers stumbled and fell onto the hard, unforgiving pavement. Arlene's screams filled Dark City, drowning the city within a city in its anxiety. "Pigs!" he yelled again. The Beretta trembled in his grip. "Damned gooks!"

"Oh, my God, no! Another flashback," Caleb said to himself. He started to round the corner to confront his friend.

"No! He's dangerous." I placed my cold hand on his chest.

"Dammit, Gabe, he's my friend."

"He will not recognize you. He saw them as … as … Vietcong. He called them 'gooks', for God's sake! For all we know, he could see us as he saw them. He's … delusional." *He needs to be put down*, Valimus whispered.

For once, I agreed with him.

****

Alfonso's hair dripped down over his face, plunging his head into shadow. The black, leather overcoat draped him like a cloak. The Beretta drooled cordite from its muzzle, ready to send death to the two mortally wounded police officers in the alley. The veteran spoke in another language; I was unsure as to what he was saying, but I knew it was an order. He motioned with the gun, making a twirling gesture.

"On your stomach!" he translated. "You will pay for what you've done." His voice was thick with emotion: pain, hate, and sorrow.

From my pocket I grabbed a throwing blade. The cross shaped steel gleamed in the streetlight.

"No," Caleb said with frost in his voice.

"I've got to stop him somehow."

"I will not let you kill my friend."

Anger spilled from my body, causing the former physician to shudder. "Do you have any suggestions?"

"Let me distract him. You can get the police officers to safety. I will stop him."

"No way. It's too dangerous." My words fell on deaf ears. As soon as the words left my mouth, Caleb rounded the corner with his arms held up.

"Alfonso? Al? It's me." His voice was as soft as a cooing mother's. The vet's body swiveled all at once. The Beretta zeroed right on the old man. I continued my rage and merged with the darkness, becoming one with it. I controlled my breathing and let the shadows envelope me, all while the cold of the dead filled the alley. A dark winter claimed Dark City.

The police officers writhed on the ground. I could tell that both had chest wounds. One of them, a tall, Hispanic man, had a lung shot. He gasped as he drowned in his own blood. The other victim had a chest wound that did not look as bad. He crawled to his partner, using the baton for leverage. He reached for his partner as I watched from the darkness.

"It's okay; it's okay." Caleb's voice soothed his demented friend.

"S-s-sarge?" Out of the corner of my eye, I noticed Alfonso's gun arm wavered.

"No, Al. It's Caleb. Do you remember me?"

"C-caleb? What are you doing in..."

"No, Al. We're not there. You're not *there*. The nightmare is gone. You will never go back to that place ever again. I promise."

The nightmare is gone, a voice echoed in my mind.

What was going on?

Whatever Valimus had up his sleeve, I did not have any time to dwell on it. Caleb was inching closer to the loose cannon and I had to make a move.

To make matters worse, the healthier cop saw his chance to exact revenge up in their injuries. With one arm, he held his partner; however, the other arm was reaching for his holstered side arm. Pain and anger makes for a deadly combination. Murder was written all over his face.

Out of sheer adrenaline, I leaped at the officers. My silver blades appeared in both hands. Even at this moment now that I have lots of time to reflect on it, I cannot recall if I blacked out or if it was an extended blink. Perhaps they are one and the same. Anyway, the next thing I remember was Caleb and four of the denizens of Dark City pulling me away from the two long dead corpses of the police officers. I can still hear the animalistic snarls that bubbled from my throat. I clawed, snapped, and thrashed. They backed away. Several of them grabbed at the fresh wounds that I had inflicted. Dark City reeked of blood; my body hummed with renewed energy. A maniacal laughter echoed within the caverns of my psyche. As I looked around, what I saw still haunts me, even as I sit in this room.

The remains of the two officers were covered in black fluid. They lay in a messy heap; their bodies never moved. Once I looked down at my bloody hands, I knew who the killer was. The tremors started in my hands and radiated outward.

A hideous laughter continued to grow in volume. But this time, it wasn't contained within my mind. It bounced off the high walls of the buildings and rattled my tonsils. It wasn't Valimus laughing.

Dear God, it came from me!

A brilliant flash of pain radiated at the base of my skull.

Then … there was nothing.

****

"Tell me about this woman." The vampire was trying to confuse me. He knew all about the woman; he probably knew more about her than I did.

"I-I don't … know her." I struggled with my jacket. It must've been laced with silver. My strength would have torn it to shreds if it wasn't. "I … can't … even *see* her."

"Do you remember her son?" His eyes were vacant, expressionless.

Then, I remembered Malfric's family and Valimus' prophecy.

"When the Indigo aura turns Midnight, the Evolution begins." I smiled.

"What does that mean to you?" He studied my gestures.

This vamp was good. Valimus sent one of his better minions, I thought. "Don't pretend with me. You know what it means. Otherwise, you wouldn't have brought up the Winthrops."

"Ah, yes, the Winthrops. Let's talk about them." He steepled his fingers again. I ground my teeth together and strained against the silver reinforced bonds of the straight jacket. He shuffled papers around on his desk and picked up a report. "Tell me about Dr. David Winthrop."

"You mean Malfric."

The vampire looked up from his papers. "I have read through your … journals. They do make for interesting reading." Everything was "interesting" to this bastard. What does that word mean? "Why do you call him that?" If he read the journals, then he knew why.

"That's his name! It was his name long before humanity existed."

"Tell me … Gabriel…" He coughed and sifted through more papers. "Why did you bury him alive in Nevada?"

"Ask him yourself!" I spat.

He adjusted his glasses and replied, "We would if he wasn't dead."

I laughed. It was clearly a lie. Malfric had survived under the sand without blood for months. The starvation must have driven him insane. If anything, Valimus must have destroyed him, knowing that he was useless. "I didn't kill him."

"If you didn't, then who did?"

"You know who. Stop playing these games."

"Ah, yes." Once again, he thumbed through his papers. "This Valimus … person."

"Enough of your damn games!" My rage took over. I struggled, but the jacket wouldn't break. I was back in the Facility, but it wasn't The Council doing the testing. It was the demon in my head.

It was Valimus!

"Calm down!" the vampire in the immaculate suit and white lab coat ordered. A burly vampire in a security guard's uniform grabbed me. His grip was a vise. The air was squeezed from me.

"You … won't get them. They will die…" I gasped for air. "They will lead me to … to…"

****

"Stoker!"

The name forced murky shadows from my mind. I sat upright but could not move my arms. They were tied to my sides by thick twine.

The stench caused me to gag. *Where am I?* I wondered. A network of pipes and brick reminded me that I was still in Dark City. My skull was on fire; whoever knocked me out put more force behind the blow than he needed to in order to render me unconscious. When you're knocked out and find yourself in a cell and bound like a victim, the first thing you want to do is yell for help. That's not a good move. I kept my calm and looked around for a way to break free of the rope. I was weak and could not force my preternatural strength to break the bonds. Plus, I knew the sun was out, which sapped my strength.

To my left, near the ceiling, was a grate, which allowed rays of light to beam through and splash against the cool, murky concrete south wall. Due to the ultraviolet radiation, The Nosferatu Virus in my veins made me yearn for sleep, but I struggled to keep my eyelids open.

A quick scan of my makeshift cell was not encouraging. A heavy steel door stood on the other side of the room. I had to find Richard Stoker. If Valimus did not want me to find this guy, then it had to mean that Stoker had valuable information on Winthrop and the enigmatic prophecy. Putting all of this together, I wondered if Stoker was Valimus' first victim. Did Stoker have the key to Valimus' past? Did he have some knowledge of how to kill this Master vampire? Once again, I struggled and raged against my ties. A roar erupted from my lips. "I need to get out of here!"

Time was of the essence.

The sounds of footfalls were faint due to the heaviness of the iron door. I shook my head to keep from falling asleep just as the soft footsteps stopped at the door. Who was on the other side of it?

My heart skipped a beat while the bolt slid back. The steel

door opened. Either it was damned heavy or whoever opening it was frail. As soon as I saw the head of Arlene poking inside, I knew the answer: both.

The timid girl eased into the room. Her eyes were as wide as a Japanese cartoon character's. She wore the same weathered clothes, faded, worn sundress, work boots, and an olive drab military jacket. Her greasy hair was pulled back into a tight ponytail. I made a point not to move at all. She was a rabbit, waiting for an excuse to hop away.

"Wh-wh-what … are you?" she whispered.

"The reason your heartbeat races when the lights go out."

"You … you drank them. Their blood." She wrapped the jacket tighter around her. "Are you a-"

"Vampire?" The word made her jump. The room filled with the scent of her fear. And it awakened the lust in me.

"Are there … monsters?" She shook her head, daring me to change her feeble notion of reality.

I nodded. "A child is very sensitive to the world that is not seen. The boogeyman, ghosts, things that go bump in the night. All of it. It's real." Her eyes lit up; intrigue and disbelief danced within them.

"You are one of *them*." I could see she wanted to step forward. She wanted to touch me to see if I was real. I nodded. Arlene stepped into a shaft of light that fell through the grate, displaying the world above. She wanted to say something. All I did was wait.

I was good at that.

"I-I hoped that things like … you … existed." Her voice was small.

"Why?"

"Because … because…" she took a deep breath as tears played along her cheeks. "If you didn't exist, then that would mean he would be considered a monster and I would be the daughter of one." She laughed, "If monsters do exist, then there is something out there worse than my dad. And I wouldn't be a monster." Her voice was a child's.

"Did he hurt you?" I shocked myself by the tenderness of my tone.

She nodded.

"Being a monster is not something that you can inherit. It is something that you are," I lied. "Just because you are related to a monster does not mean you are one. Yes, your father is a monster, but you are not." A harsh laugh trickled from my bloodstained lips. "Believe me. I know a monster when I see one. You are no monster."

A small smile creased her thin lips. Then, Arlene did something unexpected. She closed the door and sat in front of me. "Tell me about them. Tell me everything."

Perhaps it was because I was tired. Exhaustion must've gotten the better of me. Maybe it was because I was just a lonely soul who was tired of all the fighting and keeping such dark secrets. Perhaps all I wanted was for someone to listen … like I wanted with Rachel.

I nodded. "I will, but on one condition…"

****

Later that day, Arlene returned with a notepad and pencil and wrote down the names I dictated. She began writing the list of names of those I have killed, those that I have hurt, and those that I have mutilated by removing their teeth. I am not sure when my tale ended and unconsciousness began. I only remember swirling colors fading to dark, roiling blackness. Midnight flame flickered behind my eyes.

And once again, I was alive.

As if breathing for the first time, I took a long, deep breath. My eyes snapped open, wide as dinner plates. I strained against the ropes that restrained me. Something in the darkness scurried farther away. Was it a large rat? Whatever it was, it was timid, fast, and nervous.

It was used to being prey.

The smell was familiar and I remembered it.

"Who hunted you?" I asked Arlene.

"My father, among other men," came a meek reply.

"The monster."

"Yes," a whisper. "He … he … was an alcoholic." Her laugh was without mirth. "Like you." After a pause, she continued, "It changed him. Before the drink, he would be so nice and warm. But after…" she shivered.

Just like you, the demon in my head quipped.

"Shut up," I muttered.

"What?"

"We communicate through the mind. Sometimes … he speaks to me."

"Valimus?" Mentioning his name caused her to quake. Arlene soaked up the entire story. She took it all in stride, asking questions for clarification.

"Yes." Then I looked down at my ropes and the frustration returned. "Please, Arlene, let me go. I need to stop Valimus. I need to end this prophecy that may change the world as we know it."

"B-by killing … a *child*?" The look of utter confusion and horror in her eyes was the only such look I had ever seen from her at that point. Ever since she was a child, she knew monsters existed. As an adult, the notion was still within her. "But you know … it's wrong." She looked at the name Ryan Winthrop written on the list. "You know-"

"I don't know." I told her the truth. "I need to find Valimus and a man named Richard Stoker. I think Stoker is the key to this whole thing. Believe me, I don't relish the notion of killing a child. That's why I think … I hope … Stoker may be the key. If it's between killing the kid or Stoker, I'll kill Stoker."

"Do you think it'll have to come to that?"

"With the way Valimus plays games, I'm not sure at all."

Trying to switch gears, Arlene said, "So you … drink blood like they do?" She inched closer.

I nodded, remembering Jeanette Mullray, the woman trapped in a cellar with me. The Thirst drove me mad. "I have. It's not something I need to live, but it gives me strength…" I thought of the AA book in my pocket. *Just like them*, I thought. I struggled against the ropes. "With it, I could snap these ropes like they were straw."

"The blood gives you power?" She knew the answer. Why did she ask the question? The girl stepped even closer.

That did it. The scent of her skin beneath the dirt, grime and soot reawakened the lust for blood. All it took was a few, small steps. "Stay a-a-away!" I pressed against the restraints. The supernatural energy swelled against the inside of my skin. Arlene looked horrified … at first. A single heartbeat later, her eyes scanned me with an almost childlike fascination. She watched me thrash and yell. The young woman inched over the grimy floor, moving closer to me.

What she wasn't aware of was the simple fact that the ropes were wearing thin.

I would think that if most people were to see trussed up proof of an imaginary monster in the flesh, they would stop to observe it. However, with the street urchin known as Arlene, something else lay beneath the surface of the beautiful, innocuous face. Something darker. She knew that monsters existed, for her father was one of them, but she did not know the extent of that evil. Evil breeds evil. My entire life's work centered on this fact. So it stood to reason that there was a little bit of evil that dwelled within her. I do not write this to condone my actions; I struggle with this even to this day in my predicament.

Like a madman I growled. The demon that lives in me pushed to the surface. More of my rope grew weaker. Arlene's jaw dropped open. She reached a cautious hand out as if to make sure she wasn't imagining me.

"A vampire," she whispered. "So much … power." I snapped at her fingers but missed.

"G-g-get ... a-a-a..." A ragged yell tore from my cracked lips. I rebelled against my unnatural nature and warned her, but she wouldn't listen.

And now her soul is damned for it.

The audible snap was followed by her gasp. Within a blink of an eye, I was on top of her. Her chest heaved. Blood sped through her body as the fight or flight reaction screamed at her. Unfortunately, it was too late. Her body stayed frozen on the cool cement. Her eyes were wide and wild. She trembled, but not with fear. An excitement fueled her. Her lips were parted, and slightly curved in a smile that the human part of me could not comprehend, but the demon was all too familiar.

Arlene turned her neck to me. "Do it," she whispered.

I sunk my teeth into her neck. To this day, I do not remember the action. I have always wondered how I was able to bite her without severing her carotid. Why didn't I kill her? All I can recall is the stimulation of feeling her blood entering my mouth. The true undead have saliva that contains anticoagulants. It prevents clotting so the body can bleed dry, but I wasn't a full vampire ... yet. It was so difficult sucking as hard as I could to get the small amount of that precious fluid into my mouth. I had missed the major places that would have killed, my darkest parts of me didn't even want her dead. Why was this? Arlene gasped, but she held onto me! I do not know how long we held that morbid embrace before I recognized that someone was unlocking my cell door. Three people were attempting to pry us apart.

The instant my lips were disengaged from her neck, I was a ferocious animal. With a roar, I lashed out at the men nearby. The humanity that dwelled within me was far away. Now, I recall the moments after I fell off the wagon ... again, but that is only in dreams. Caleb was towards the door pleading for me to stop. He rushed towards the prone woman, who moaned and clutched her neck.

Tim, the stocky man with the wool cap, eyed me with cold orbs. He held a length of pipe and stood in a crouch. Two other men flanked him. At the time, they were just pieces of meat that blocked my way towards the exit. Caleb's voice was the only thing my far away humanity could respond to. He pulled Arlene to a corner of the room and held her while trying to talk sense into me.

"Gabriel, it's okay. We can help you. Y-you are sick." He said more things, but they only come back to me in my dreams. "…identity disorder … cure…"

"Cure?" I yelled, but it only came out as a growl. "There is no cure." They did not understand what I was saying. I could only speak in animalistic screeches.

One of the two men with Tim charged forward. As usual, I reacted to the movement violently. When Tim and the other guard watched as their comrade tumbled across the room, they gave me more space.

"Gabriel!" Caleb's yell pushed the demon back. It saved the two men's lives. I looked over at the doctor. "You are sick." The words struck a chord; maybe it's because I believed him. "I am a doctor. I mean, I was a doctor."

"You still are," I said. Again, it came out as a long, low growl. Why could I not speak? Was the demon inside of me so feral, that it controlled *everything* about me?

"Let me help you."

My humanity ached at the desperation in his voice. Arlene groaned in the doctor's arms and turned her head to look at me. She held a slip of blood spattered paper in her hand. The young woman handed the paper to Caleb and whispered in his ear. I backed towards the door. Tim closed in on me. I moved closer. He showed me the craftiness in his eyes; I knew he was getting ready to strike. Hissing at him, I reached into my coat pocket for a weapon.

I was unarmed.

My hiss grew, radiating frustration. So much was going on that it overloaded my senses. That was when the homeless man lunged. He thrust at me but did not reach me.

"Stop!" Caleb stood up and held the bloody paper in his hands. "Gabriel, you're a good man with a good soul, no matter what you may think." He held the paper out towards me. "Remember our talks. You believe in your recovery. You have made a list and you want to atone for your sins. If you take a step in the wrong direction, your soul *will* be lost." I knew he was right. It caused the monster in me to pause. "You aren't a monster. You are a man holding onto his humanity. I know where you're coming from. I've been there."

Valimus was screaming in my head. He spoke of violence, death, chaos. I knew that the demon in my mind was my addiction. I was on the edge of sanity. It wouldn't take much to send me over. To save the men and woman in the cell, I did the only thing my body would allow. I ran for the exit. As I brushed past the men ready to pounce, I looked back. It was a split second, but it was enough to make me question: Why was Arlene holding onto one of the men's left foot. A split second later, I plunged through the doorway and into the abyss beneath the city. Unfortunately, I knew that they would pursue me. They were searching for me, but I knew it wouldn't take them very long to regret their decision.

If Dark City was a maze, then the sewers beneath the city were the ultimate labyrinth. My run through the confined length of tunnel was made that much more difficult by the ankle-deep waters through which I sloshed. The faint sounds of receding footsteps and echoing voices pursued me, spurring me further into the shadows.

Why are you running? Valimus echoed. *You could kill them and no one would even give a damn! They are the perfect victims.*

"That is why I am running."

A side tunnel led me away from the watery passageway to drier ground. It was a slight incline and I hid behind an outcropping. All I could hear was my raspy breathing. The taste of Arlene was still on my lips. By the time I finished wiping her life from my lips, my pursuers were mere yards away. Voices echoed along the narrow walls of the sewer system.

"Where did he go?" Tim asked.

"It's like he vanished," the other man replied. "Did you see what he did to those cops? To Arlene?"

"Not sure which is worse: What he did or what *we* did?"

"Had to do it, Tim. You know just as well as I do what would've happened if the cops found their bodies. Dark City would be burnt to a crisp."

"Yeah, I know. But…" He looked around.

"The bodies'll be washed out to sea. Nobody will find them." While they had me locked in the sewer room, they had disposed of the bodies of the police officers I had killed. They were survivors, just like me. A part of me felt guilty for thinking of them as my victims. Already, the line between predator and prey became blurry.

I followed my pursuers, as they waded through the muck. Crawling along a ledge ten feet above them, I observed them with a cool detachment. Tim was a fighter, but he knew nothing of stalking. Neither of them knew enough to keep their mouths shut.

But I did.

Valimus continued to whisper seductive horrors into my ear, as if he spoke from the very shadows that contained me.

Kill them. Taste their blood as you did hers.

I shivered at the thought. Reaching for the AA book that I shared with Caleb, another fellow addict, I slid my fingers along the worn spine.

"'God, grant me the serenity to accept the things I cannot change; the courage to change the things I can; and the wisdom to know the difference.'" The whispered prayer swirled around me.

You've become a monster, Gabriel. Praying isn't for monsters. Your soul is already damned. He continued to whisper dark passions. And in those passions were my desires. Then, I realized something so dangerous that it changed the whole game.

I was not strong *enough*.

With an inhuman growl, I sprang from the darkness. The man with Tim screamed, but his cry was cut short as I tore his throat out with my bare teeth. Blood showered my face. His neck exploded, bathing me in ecstasy.

Tim swung his pipe at me. It glanced along my arm, rendering it useless. I took a swipe at him. My fingers dug into the stocky homeless man's face. He screamed and stumbled backwards. The nameless, throatless bum gurgled in the black waters of the sewer. His eyes settled into a cold, glassy stare. The stocky man stared at his friend and screamed anew.

"P-please..." Tears streamed from his beady eyes. "Don't kill me." He looked up into my black eyes. Standing over him with blood draining from my face, I must have looked exactly like the devil that I was. There was no forgiveness in my heart. There was no compassion in my soul, assuming I had one at that point.

"Gabriel ... please. I'll say that you ... you gave me the slip." Tim's lower lip trembled. Spittle frothed the edges of his mouth. "Please don't kill-"

I never gave him a chance to finish the thought. Tim died screaming. His was a slow, agonizing death that seemed to take a long time coming. By the time I was finished, my arms were exhausted and bits of my victim floated away in the black sewer waters. His screams continued to echo along the walls long after he took his last, pain-filled gasp. At first, I wondered why no one came to help him. Who would want to run *towards* a person being torn to pieces? Not even the heroic Caleb came to rescue his charge.

As I allowed the shadows to consume me as I did Tim; I glanced at a reflection of a monster in the waters. I knew the truth. I had come to Culver's Bay to find a monster. I was concerned that this beast was the most powerful creature I had ever faced. And clearly, I had found it.

It was the kind of monster that made kids hide under blankets, and cause men to continue screaming long after their deaths.

This demon was *me*.

A chuckle started low in my stomach. Then, it grew and grew.

And grew.

A demonic cackle thundered throughout the sewer system as the last vestige of my humanity receded into the oblivion.

And the demon was released, completely and unrestrained.

****

The demon stalked the sewers. It ran through the darkness and splashed amid the ankle-deep murkiness. It did not care about being quiet or cautious.

All it wanted was another fresh kill.

Bits of Tim slipped from beneath its fingernails and fell from its slimy maw. It moved by instinct alone, traversing the darkness with reckless abandon. It enjoyed being free. *I* enjoyed being unrestrained.

The Darkness within me filled my body, a cold chill, frostier than any arctic evening, poured from my beating heart into the rest of my insides. I rode the Evil like a bucking bronco, yearning to be tamed.

Or was it me that was being tamed?

I did not know where I began and It ended, nor did I care.

It rounded a corner; a flickering light drew its attention. The creature followed the light like the proverbial moth. As it rounded more corners, the light pushed back the darkness. I continued to follow it until I found myself in a hidden cramped room. Candles sat atop rickety tables with fading wood in various stages of decay.

Adorned on the cement walls were glorious works of art. All of them were painted in bold, dark colors. Reds, blacks, deep blues. Heavy, deep strokes slid along the thick canvases. I stared at a portrait of a nude woman curled in the corner of the room. A menacing shadow fell over her horrified face. I stepped closer to the picture and smelled the canvas. The scent was familiar.

It was Arlene.

The paintings conveyed one single emotion: fear. Another painting was a closeup of a blond haired woman peering around a corner. She stared at me with eyes of pure dread.

It felt so … normal!

But something was not "normal." Something was amiss. I wasn't alone. My eyes were slits. Looking around, I knew some *thing* stayed in the deep shadows that were splashed across the walls. Why could I not see into them?

I growled and turned around.

If I had not done so, I would've been killed.

A bullet sheared a portion of my left ear away. Later, I found out that the earlobe was blown off. I screamed and lost my balance. The water was cold but seemed even worse when my face smashed through the surface. The chill sent shards through my face, putting me with its rawness.

As I pulled my head from the waters, the gunshot continued to echo through the tunnels. Multiple booming clicks filled my brain.

"Dammit!" the voice was tinged with hysteria.

Alfonso, Valimus echoed in my head.

Knowing he was out of ammo, I let the beast take over. I leaped from the cold waters and spun towards him. An evil roar exploded from my lungs through the tube. Our bodies collided in the dark. The wind was forced from his lungs. I fell atop him; my fingers found their way to his throat. Will all of the strength I could muster, I throttled him. Most of his head was submerged, but his face stood above the water. His eyes rolled around in his head, lips were slightly opened.

I never saw the movement, but it felt like the side of my head collapsed. Pain shot through my face, numbed my skull and tilted the world. The combat vet threw me aside and stumbled to his feet. He held my Beretta at his side.

Not my Beretta, I thought. Briefly, I recalled the cop I had taken it from. He was just doing his job, but he was infected.

"Nothin' personal." My speech was slurred.

"Wha-?" Alfonso looked confused. I couldn't be distracted by mistakes. I had to react.

I ran headlong at my prey. It was difficult to move through ankle-deep water. The homeless man may have been crazy, but he was not slow. He lunged to one side and pounded me with a falling elbow to the center of my back.

Pathetic, the monster I lived with taunted me.

"Your kind is good at fighting in the dark!" he growled.

He was still in Vietnam. He was in a world that no longer existed.

I pitied and envied him.

I pitied his ignorance of reality. He was disengaged from the world around him, much like you who question *our* existence. Yet, I envied that naiveté. He was clueless to the "paranormal." He did not worry about us.

Still, he had to die.

No one could stand in my way of … of…

The insane vet kicked me in the ribs. "I'm not going to let you kill us anymore!" His voice was shaky. I crawled to my feet and watched him weep. "I watched as you killed friend after friend until every person I cared about was wiped from the face of this God forsaken planet!"

"Alfonso, it wasn't me that killed your friends." Could he listen to reason? "I am so sorry. I too lost people I cared about." *Who?* I wondered. My pain was akin to his own. I could feel it.

"No!" He held his hands to the sides of his skull, to drown out my logic. "You took them away. My friends. *My wife.*" His legs quaked. "*M-m-my … son.*" They gave out and he fell to his knees.

And that was when I struck!

I inched towards the broken man. Salivating at the easy kill, I moved closer. Quick movements always scared away the prey. A predator needs to be slow and calm. It was the best way to lull the target into a false sense of relaxation.

Then, the trap is sprung!

As I stood over him, he trembled with an all-consuming sorrow. He could not keep from crying. I knew the best way to silence those tears. I could end that suffering forever.

All I had to do was what came so seductively natural to me.

So I did it.

I hugged him to my chest.

When he began talking, I merely listened.

He told the sad story of a father, his son, and his wife.

****

Once upon a time, there lived a small family…

There was a mommy, a daddy, and a baby boy. And during that once upon a time, they were happy…

Until the baby boy grew older.

Daddy noticed that the boy was not like normal children. His son would tell him that there were things he could see that no one else could. He would dream of events that would happen days later. He would see people who were already dead.

Daddy was disturbed.

Mommy and Daddy took their withdrawn son to counseling. But the therapist merely said that their son had an overactive imagination.

"He's creative, Rick." Mommy said after going to their third therapist. "Maybe we're making this out to be more than it is."

"There is something wrong with our son and I'm not supposed to panic? This is not normal, Susan!" Daddy didn't know it, but his son was listening to their conversation. He always did when they fought. Eric felt more comfortable talking to Mommy about his strange dreams. She was comforting and nurturing.

Daddy was different.

Daddy was cold, aloof, and distant. Eric knew his father loved him. All fathers loved their sons, right? Yet, Daddy was different.

He wasn't like the other kids' daddies.

During the nights, Daddy would stay up late, reading in the study. He read book after book of psychology. Eric would sneak downstairs and peer through the slit in the door and watched as Daddy stared at his books. He would make notes in a book he wasn't allowed to touch. One day the son touched the worn spine and Daddy spanked him hard. Mommy yelled at Daddy for days afterward. Soon things were back to normal.

For a month.

Daddy studied psychology even more, but after a few months, his interests turned to the occult. He would read on myths, legends, demons, and even legitimate "paranormal research."

He would talk to Mommy about something called Indigo Children. These were children with "gifts." Daddy would ask his son many questions, which Eric answered with glee. The boy was happy that Daddy was spending time with him, so he would answer all of the questions like the good little boy that he was. Daddy would call him a "good boy" and would take him out for ice cream.

On a cold, rainy night, Mommy and Daddy were asleep. The boy snuck down the stairs and into Daddy's study. He saw Daddy's book lying on the desk. It was big and had a leather cover. It looked old. It held all of Daddy's secrets; he knew it. This could tell him what was wrong with him. Why did he "see" things? What was an Indigo Child? Were they bad?

The boy touched the book and gasped. He knew it was Daddy's Secret Book, but he had to look. After all, it was about him.

Thunder cracked the world like a whip. A flash of lightening lit up the night. The boy jumped when he saw his father standing in the corner of the room. His eyes were flat, glassy.

"You know, don't you?" he asked in a monotone.

"What do you mean, Daddy? I'm sorry. I just want to know if you knew what's wrong with me."

For a split second, the boy watched the hurt in his father's eyes. "Y-you're…" he took a deep breath. "You're perfect, my son. There is nothing wrong with you." Daddy went to his knees and extended his arms. *"You're perfect just the way you are."* With tears in his eyes, the boy hugged his father in the way every son wants to hug his dad. He could not remember a moment when he had ever felt such happiness, such freedom.

"I'm ... okay?"

"You're perfect. You're my son."

Both of them closed their eyes, feeling that moment forever.

But Daddy held his son at arm's length and smiled. "You go to bed. I'll be up to tuck you in soon." With a wide smile, his son nodded and ran to the stairs.

"I love you, Daddy," Eric said.

"I love you, son," Richard replied.

Eric ran to his room as Daddy opened a cabinet near the desk in the study.

He retrieved a 12-gauge shotgun and loaded shells inside...

****

After listening to Alfonso's story, I continued to hold the man to my chest, but he was heavy, so heavy. I opened my eyes and stared into the homeless man's eyes. They were gazing off into space over my head. His eyes and chest were unmoving.

I laid his cold body into the dark waters. His neck hung at an awkward angle. I could not remember when I broke his neck, but due to the serene look on his face, I knew neither would he.

If he had truly killed his family as he said he did, then I was doing him a favor. I knew he felt such pain and remorse over his horrific action. I was relieving him from his suffering.

"May God have mercy on your soul," I whispered not sure if I was referring to him or myself.

****

While lurking in the sewers of Culver's Bay, my mind was racing. I was thinking of Alfonso's family, my mission, Rachel, and a ton of other things. Through all of my quandaries, one thing kept coming back to me: *indigo children*. There was something familiar about that. But what? What did Alfonso have to do with my mission? He seemed to be a man with a psychological disorder and nothing more, but there was something so familiar about the indigo children.

Indigo. Indigo. *Indigo!* "That's it!" My voice echoed down the tunnels.

All of a sudden, the echoes of explosions and screams filled the tunnels.

"On your knees!" came an authoritative shout.

"Down! Down!"

Without another thought, I ran through the dank tube. I knew the police would be cracking down on Dark City. They would be looking for their missing brothers. With the chaos that I have been raising, I'm sure Agent Andrews would not be far behind. I barely survived one encounter with him. I wasn't relishing another.

Andrews. My thoughts shifted to the federal agent. Why was he so intent on capturing me? The broadcast I watched from inside Rachel's apartment, that night, told me that he was a fed and was following me across the country. Seeing the rage in his eyes up close and personal, not to mention being on the other end of his gun, told me to be afraid of him.

Gun. Gun. Gun. The Beretta. My gun was still clutched in the icy grip of the dead combat veteran. I had no weapons to protect myself. The police were probably going through my gun bag full of weapons and the satchel of extracted teeth from vampires. Caleb's family had confiscated my blades before they locked me in the sewer. It wouldn't take a genius to know that it would be so easy to pin my war with the undead on these poor people as well.

How many lives have I ruined?

I can't worry about that now, I thought as I heard manhole covers being opened several yards away. *I'll make things right after I get to the bottom of this whole prophecy thing.*

Thanks to Alfonso, I knew just where to go.

And I didn't like it one bit.

****

It took me two hours to reach the surface and ditch the dragnet that descended over Dark City. That emotion Caleb made me feel returned with a vengeance. Helplessness mingled with fury while I watched Caleb being led to a cruiser in handcuffs. Our eyes met before his head was lowered into the squad car. His eyes held a profound sorrow that I had never seen in anyone before. He had a piece of bloody paper in his hand that no one seemed to see. Holding my gaze, he nodded at me and dropped the paper to the pavement. I stood on the edge of a rooftop as a police chopper with a sweeping spotlight passed. The artificial light splashed over the claustrophobic landscape. Two officers pulled a long plastic bag out of the sewer. *Was it Tim, his companion, or Alfonso?* I wondered grimly.

Keeping to the shadows, I worked my way to the street and away from Dark City. Away from my helplessness.

Away from my fear.

I stole a Hyundai and headed east. Three miles later, I parked the vehicle behind the brownstone apartment complex where Rachel lived. By the time I climbed the fire escape and sat outside her home, she was sitting in her bedroom talking on her cell phone.

"The dreams are still coming. I-I see a man. He … kills people and…" Her voice trailed off as the drizzling rain grew more intense. Once I was able to press my ear against the cold pane of glass, I could hear her conversation. "…not sure why. I'm not drinking or using anymore. The pills are helping me sleep and they are making the dreams come less frequently." She paused and nodded. "Yes, it disturbs me! I've been dreaming shit like this *all* my life! I see him again and again." The beautiful woman grew restless. She began pacing the room, taking deep breaths. "Yes. Yes, I-" She looked at her front door. "Someone's at the door. I have to go." The addict disconnected the call and headed out of the room. Luckily, she left her window ajar. I lifted the pane upward, but only slightly.

"Who are you?" her voice drifted back to me. The other voice was even more muffled. "Can I see some ID?" Alarm bells exploded in my brain. I swore aloud as another familiar voice danced towards me.

"Thank you for allowing me to see you at such an hour." Agent Jack Andrews' voice was balanced, professional.

"What can I help you with?" There was a faint tremor in Rachel's pitch. It contained a hint of caution.

"Have you seen this man?" My heart beat sped up. I knew he had shown her an image of my face.

"What's it to you?"

"Please, Ms. Rice, this is a serious investigation. This man is wanted for a string of murders that have occurred across the country."

"Wh-what?"

"If you don't talk to me, you should know that you are hampering an active federal investigation, which could make you an accessory. This could make you eligible, but not limited to-"

"I get it! I get it! But that's not the name I know him as."

"This was taken several years ago and may be an alias."

"He looked different, but I think it was him. He goes by Gabe."

"Gabriel Brimstone?"

"I don't know."

"I have it on good authority that he frequented an Alcoholics Anonymous meeting. A meeting you attend."

"How? Who? That's confidential!" Anger warmed the air.

"It doesn't matter, Ms. Rice. Do you know where he is?"

She sighed. "No, I don't."

"Ms. Rice, you could be charged with aiding and abetting a known fugitive if you aren't telling us everything you know."

"I'm telling you everything!" she exclaimed. "He told the group when he joined that he was just in town for a few weeks and that his family was dead. He's probably staying in a motel somewhere. I don't know."

The agent replied, "There is a motel, we have traced him to, but he hasn't been there in weeks."

Weeks? Had it really been that long?

"He keeps to himself. I haven't seen him at a meeting in a while." There was silence. The hissing of the pouring rain eased my nerves like a cobra would. "Do you really think Gabe did this?" Her voice was fragile.

"You don't know the man I've been tracking for years. He is a vicious, cold-blooded murderer."

"He's also an addict. He's looking for someone to help him."

"Here is my card," the agent said. "Just be careful. Every person he has come across has fallen victim to his paranoia and delusions. He places them in a world of monsters and demons and turns them into the creatures. Then, he destroys them." I heard the door slam shut. Moments later, Rachel appeared in the bedroom, threw herself onto the bed in front of me and cried.

I nearly threw open the window and grabbed the lovely addict. Instead, I placed my palm against the cool glass. It didn't seem to be enough, but it was all I could do … for now. I wanted to hold her to my chest and tell her that what the FBI agent was saying was not true. It is true that I killed a lot of monsters, but they weren't human.

Until recently.

Valimus watched me from the reflection in the glass. His venomous smile injected fire through my veins. *That is not me!* my mind raged. *It is what he wants you to believe.* Laughter filled my brain. Valimus was getting the upper hand. He made me fall off the wagon. He made me kill humans. He made me an enemy of the world I sought to protect.

My revenge would be to end the prophecy.

It finally made sense to me.

When the indigo aura turns midnight, the Evolution begins. I thought of Alfonso's confession. He knew that his child was an Indigo Child. He knew what he had to do. Yes, it made him a monster, but he was doing what he knew was right. At least he had the guts to do it, right?

Looking at the crying woman and the reflection of Valimus in the glass, I knew I would have to act quickly.

He could not have the Indigo Children, the special ones who were in tune with the supernatural. It was why Alfonso killed his son and went crazy. He could not live in this reality. His reality was Vietnam.

"I'm sorry, Rachel." I eased up the window.

She had to die.

Before I could lift the window any further, another soft knock at her door distracted me. Rachel got up from her bed and rushed over to the door.

"Hayes, what are you doing here?" I sensed something between them the moment I attended the meetings.

"I was just … worried about you." He seemed timid, as if he was unsure of her response.

"A fed just left, can you believe that?" There was another pause. "Wait a minute. Do you know anything about that?" Another pause. "You were the one who talked to him about Gabe, didn't you?"

"Rachel, please! Just hear me out for a second."

"You did!" Her voice grew louder. She appeared in the doorway to the bedroom and snatched a packet of cigarettes off the night stand. "Gabe may not be who he says he is, but he *is* an addict. Just like you and me. We come to these meetings so we can work through our addictions in open environments, without judgment and with those like us. I cannot believe you would-"

"He's a damned killer! He's killed all over this country. I cannot allow a killer to hide among us."

"Who the hell are you to pass judgment on one of us? How do you know that for certain?" She stabbed a finger against his chest.

"Rachel, please-"

"The hell with you!"

"Rachel, I-I…" He grabbed her wrists and pulled her to him. He smashed his lips against hers. She slipped out of his grip and slapped him across the face.

"Bastard! Is this why you did it? Were you jealous that I talked to Gabe a couple times? What kind of asshole are you?"

"Listen to me. I love you. As soon as I saw you-"

"No!" She lashed out again, but that time, Hayes Sanders blocked her slap and pushed her against the bed.

"Please," he repeated over and again. He fell atop Rachel as her body hit the mattress. "You've got to listen to me."

"Get off of me!" she screamed. He would not go away. His desires took over. Any addict would know about that.

So I knew I couldn't let him get away with it.

The window exploded when my booted foot shot through it. I followed the glass inward and grappled with Sanders, who happened to be an agile man. He grabbed my shoulders and pushed back.

"Gabe!" Rachel screamed and rolled away from the bed and flying shards.

"You made a big mistake," I growled at the AA host. He pushed me against a dresser that was next to the broken window. I rocked his head with an uppercut beneath the chin. He grunted and loosened his grip, but I didn't lose mine. I yanked him closer to me and hit him again. Sanders stumbled backwards like a drunk.

I knew he was dead the moment I stepped into the room. It was as inevitable as the dawn cresting in a few hours. Rachel was unaware of this. "Gabe, no!" she yelled in the background, but she might as well have been ten miles away. I had him on the ropes and I wasn't going to back away. *It* was coming to the surface and it was *so* easy to let the damned thing take over.

So that was what I did.

With a roar, I flung him across the room. Sanders slammed against the opposite wall. His face was contorted in pain.

126

"G-G-G-" He couldn't even get my name out of his lips. The poor victim raised his hands to protect his face, but it was all in vain. I rushed across the room and continued to pummel him.

"Gabe!" Rachel shrieked again.

I didn't listen. Over and over I smashed my meaty fists against Hayes' face, and again Rachel called my name. She cried and begged for me to stop. After many seconds, the would-be rapist stopped screaming. The sweet aroma of his bloody, broken face could not stop me from beating him. A part of me knew he was dead, but I didn't stop.

Then Rachel said something that made my blood run cold. She said two words that made my world come to a sudden halt.

"Richard Stoker!"

I swiveled my body to face her. The smell of Hayes Sanders' blood drooling down my arm was a distant memory.

"Wh-what did you call me?"

"Richard Stoker. That's what the fed that visited me called you. You look so different now than you did in that picture."

Then, I recalled my first encounter with Agent Andrews. He seemed to have seen me before. What did he know about me?

"Why did you do it?"

"To protect you." Did I? Why would I want to protect her when I was at her window to kill her?

She looked at the bloody remnants of Hayes' skull and shuddered. "Why did you kill all of these people?"

"To protect you," I repeated. "You have powers no normal person should have. I have come to end a suffering that people like you have had for a long time. They would have used you for their purposes, but I just want to end your pain. I know what it's like to-" I inched closer to her, but she recoiled.

"Don't you *dare* touch me!" she yelled. "What do you know about suffering?"

"I am not normal, *either*."

She laughed at that. "That's for sure." She kept several feet between us at all times. "A-are you a ... a killer?"

"Would you believe me if I told you?"

"Try me," she replied with ice in her veins.

"I'm not insane. And I'm *not* Richard Stoker."

"Oh yeah? Well, Agent Andrews showed me a picture that looked an awful lot like you."

Lies! Valimus screamed in my mind. *Don't believe her! You need to kill her. That is why I sent you that message. Your world will fall apart if she lives. The whole world will fall apart if she lives. Her kind deserves to die!*

"You lie," I growled at her. "You do nothing but lie." It all made sense. Once again, I took a back seat to *It* and let the beast take over.

"Gabe-"

"Shut up!" The beast smacked her across her face. "Gabriel Brimstone is gone!" It approached her prone form and grabbed her wrists, pinning her to the carpet. "Just call me ... Valimus!" It laughed as It tore out Rachel's neck. The beast looked at the window and saw my reflection smiling a bloody grin back at it.

And deep, in the back of his psyche, Gabriel Brimstone screamed.

****

Dawn caught me unawares. The beast was asleep, leaving me to wrestle with my demons. There was so many of them that I lost count.

I stared into the window of a bakery. My stubbly beard and sunken cheeks looked different from the man in the Wanted poster that Agent Andrews had given Rachel, but there was no denying the resemblance. I remembered seeing the picture she'd referred to mere moments after I had killed her. It lay on the plush carpeting near the doorway. I shuddered at the accusatory look in her eyes.

Valimus was right all along. Finding Richard Stoker spelled the end of me.

Looking into the dead, vacant eyes of the homeless man in the window, I saw many people: Richard Stoker, the family man who lost everything; Gabriel Brimstone, half man, half vampire, and defender of humanity; and Valimus, a demented, seductive vampire looking to amass untold power to trigger an evolution of humanity. Was I all of these people? Was I none of them? Was I simply the transient that the middle-class passersby thought that I was?

Or was I the serial killer that the press called The Tooth Fairy that everyone thought I was?

I continued to stay away from the main streets. My disheveled clothes and terrible odor allowed me to blend in with other homeless survivors on the street. I stayed with them and foraged for food. Several of us stood in front of a dumpster and I watched while they dug into the garbage bin and talked.

"So did you hear what happened in Dark City last night?" A man with an overgrown beard stuffed a half-eaten sandwich into his dirty face.

"You mean the maniac that killed Caleb's family?" Another guy, a tall man with long, thin arms found a packet of mustard and opened it. He sucked the condiment down his throat. "Damn shame. He was a good man. Hear he's in jail now. Heard he killed some cops or something."

"No, it wasn't him. It was the demon." The man with the furry face whispered. His eyes were wide with fear.

"Richie, you've been drinking too much Wild Turkey. That's bull and you know it."

"No. It's true. I heard he came in the form of a man who needed help. You know how Caleb is about taking in strays. So this guy comes and stays with him and he ends up killing Al, Tim, and Marc."

"What about Arlene? She was real cute." The tall man licked his lips.

"I heard that from Arlene herself," Richie said. I tried not to look interested. I continued to forage around in the dumpster but could not find anything. Richie continued, shaking his head. "That girl's in a bad way. I have a feeling that she won't last long. She looks like she's got the flu or something. You know how bad those things can get, 'specially since it's so close to winter."

"Don't believe that girl." He jumped into the dumpster and looked deeper into the bin. "That girl's looney tunes. I heard she said something about that demon too. She was talking about how he helped her see the world for what it was."

My mind raced at the possibility of her telling others about the existence of the undead. If she told anyone what really lurked in the dark, she would be a target by the monsters. I couldn't let that happen!

I took off down an alleyway, looking for an entrance to the sewer system.

****

It took me an hour, but I found the section of the tunnel where I was the night before. With painstaking slowness, I made my way to my former cell. The room was empty; the only clue that something was amiss was the yellow police tape that restricted the area. This place was still a crime scene, but it was such a cesspool for contamination that whatever the crime scene investigators could find would be tainted.

Beneath the city was a whole world that few people acknowledged. I had been through enough sewers stalking the prey of the Nightside so many times that it seemed like second nature to ease through these sewers.

Really? the voice in my head laughed. *After what you know now? After your entire world has crashed in on itself? What are you doing now? Are you really looking for devils in the darkness, or are you chasing a figment of your own imagination? If you are chasing ghosts that live inside of your mind, then what does that make me? Am I Valimus, or am I something else? Am I your conscience? If that's the case, then why am I telling you to stay in your fake world where it's safe and you aren't a homicidal maniac? Would a conscience tell you that?*

I could not block out the thoughts as they crashed through my cerebral cortex. The walls of an entire reality/world had caved in on me within less than twenty-four hours. I was broken. My mind was following a script I knew was fake, and I was just going through the motions. Reality was a movie and I was watching what events would unravel in front of me. My motions were on auto-pilot and there was little I could do to salvage my life.

There was little I could do to save Rachel.

It took a lot of searching, but I found the small, hidden room where Arlene kept her paintings. It reminded me of one of those Hammer horror films. The fading lights of the worn candles cast shadows along the walls. The morbid canvases looked even scarier in the dim light. The police had not found this little hidden room. They had not found this fortress for a meek woman with a darkness that was infecting her soul. Her fear had manifested and was taking control of her. I searched the room for that list I had given her. My list of those I needed to apologize to.

To those I had wronged.

Rachel had known of its existence. I needed that list. I looked for the slip of paper but could not find it. My list and hopes were dashed and with it went my thoughts of salvation.

Step Nine

"Made direct amends to such people wherever possible, except when to do so would injure them or others."

Being a transient did have· its advantages. No one really sees them. Who tries to remember the face of a bum? You don't care about them. No one looked at me while I panhandled for spare change. It was the perfect cover while I cased The Milton Center for Mental Health. Plus, it was the perfect way to sum up how I felt. I didn't want to be noticed. I wanted to be left alone, to brood about my tragic revelation and the task that was to come.

While I stood inside the parking ramp structure across the street, I couldn't help but think that I had come full circle but accomplished nothing. The cup of tepid coffee in my hand tasted like distilled motor oil, but it was the only thing that seemed real to me. I was not sure who I was or if what I was doing was even real.

So why was I intent on finishing this dream?

I suppose someone could understand me finishing the fantasy if I was successful at it. I was failing as a recovering addict. My "addiction" to blood wasn't kicked. I had lost the list of people to whom I wanted to make amends. I had slaughtered hundreds of people, all in the name of a war that wasn't even real. Not even Don Quixote had it this bad. At least his dragons were harmless windmills.

One of my windmills happened to be Rachel Rice, a gifted person who would become the perfect weapon in the hands of a vampire. By killing her, I foiled Valimus' plans. There was one more Indigo Child that I had to kill: Ryan Winthrop, son of the piece of garbage bloodsucker I had thought I killed long ago. Since Ryan was already half-vamp like me, I would have to take more drastic measures in eliminating that child. Part of me screamed at me to stop this madness. The forensic psychologist at my trial testified that in his meetings with me, I was fully aware of the difference between right and wrong, but my reality was different from others. That distinction saved me from the death penalty; at least that's what I heard. To this day, I still wonder if I am in the reality that you know, or my own version of reality. Still, I think of Ryan Winthrop and my grim mission. Could I do it? Was harming a child worth keeping an illusion that I knew deep down was just that?

The thought of what I had to do made me nauseous. Yet, though all of that, I was patient. I waited. For days I lived in that parking ramp, learning the placement of the security cameras and how they moved on their swivel posts. It took me a long time to learn where to stand, how long to stand in that position and places in the shadows hidden from the cameras. I would emerge from my new home to grab supplies that would help me in my task. In the dank, murky depths I only had the voice of Valimus to keep me company. I would like to think that I hung onto the last vestiges of my sanity, but that was too optimistic for my liking. I watched myself whisper to the demon in my head, telling me seductive stories that I bought into because I was so weak willed. It was all too easy to wrap myself up in the dream. The cold, hard reality of it was too difficult to face. It was difficult to face the fact that I was a family man who saw remnants of his own latent insanity passed onto my own son. In that fear, I grabbed a shotgun and ended the lives of my family and escaped from the law, from responsibility, and from reality by staying in the confines of my fractured psyche. No, I didn't want to believe that.

So I stayed.

I returned to being the hero ... who wasn't. I stayed being the vigilante, the anti-hero, the lone wolf. That was easier. It was easier to do something as heinous as what I was intent on doing. I would rather do that than face life. Life is hard. It's why children enjoyed pretending...it's why Eric enjoyed...

As the hours turned into days, Valimus told stories of darkness, devils, and eternal torment. He reminded me of why I had to kill this victim and others. *What does it mean to be truly innocent in a world like this?* he asked. *A man who would have an affair with his friend's wife, even if he is dead ... does this man deserve to live? A woman who would forsake her husband, even if he has been gone ... should she die? You know how children get. Remember when you saw Eric pulling the wings off of butterflies and burning ants with a magnifying glass? How long would it have taken for him to change into a monster? "Boys just being boys" is that it? That's what they all say. Killers like Gacy, Gein, Dahmer, and Bundy began the same way.* For days I listened to his dark phantasms, *my* dark phantasms, our dark phantasms. And I hated myself for it.

I pushed away my self-loathing and opened a copy of that day's issue of *The Culver's Bay Gazette* that I found on the grimy concrete floor. I read a story of the slaughter in the sewers of Culver's Bay. Beneath that story was another story of the police still unable to find the culprit called The Tooth Fairy. They had found his sack of teeth from the bloody motel room with the mutilated corpses that were recent victims of the maniac. *My* sack of teeth. They were in police custody and the feds were waiting for a lead on me. Try as I might, I could not shake the feeling of foreboding doom that overwhelmed me. I returned to the story of the vicious cannibal that had torn through the subterranean caverns and knew that this killer was me.

I continued reading the paper. The reporter interviewed several of the homeless and they told stories of a demon that walked the sewers at night. This demon would take a victim each night and has been doing so for the past three days. During those days, I have been in the parking ramp.

"Still think I'm making this up, Andrews?" I asked the shadows, and Valimus. As usual, they didn't respond. "I'll deal with you later," I said to the newspaper. I pushed back the guilt I felt. I knew who this monster was. I had unleashed it onto the city; someone else was infected with my delusion. Reading this propelled me further into my delusions. My insanity was infecting your reality. I knew the best way to deal with this was to complete my mission. It had to be.

So I returned to the moment, returned to my reality that was seeping into your reality. *Focus!* I knew my prey would approach sooner or later, so I waited. The waiting gave me time to think … and plan.

A length of pipe was taped to the side of my right leg. Using a brick, I shaped a sheet of steel and wedged it against my chest using my belt, and not to mention my little break-in of a survival store. Two hunting knives with belts, gloves, and new boots would work well in my plan.

Plan? It asked. We smiled.

Andrews' sedan stopped at the curb in front of the building. He exited the car and milled about in the little courtyard in front of the building. I raced down the stairs to the street. Time was of the essence.

I experienced déjà vu as I emerged onto terra firma. A semi, resembling the one that killed the suicidal vampire that I tried to intimidate, blurred by. Part of me wondered if it was really a vampire instead of some hapless person who was being chased by a maniac. Perhaps his fear caused him to run into the path of the oncoming semi. As I looked up into the sky, I watched ash rained onto the street. It disappeared as soon as I blinked. The ash rains in a different reality.

My eyes stayed fixed on the federal agent while I crossed the busy road. I shuffled into the shadows of a looming building and ruffled through a nearby trash can. My eyes continued to stay riveted on the agent.

Why are you still doing this? Why are you playing this futile game? I wondered who was doing the talking but knew that it didn't matter. I was Valimus and he was me. I was a dog chasing its own tail. I committed carnage and then set out to avenge it. I was the mass murderer that the media and police made me out to be.

I was the Tooth Fairy.

I thought of the woman I had attacked. "Yes, Arlene, there are monsters." To whomever reads this tome, if you think these are the ravings of a madman, or if somewhere in the deepest, darkest part of your subconscious, there lies some sanity, one thing is clear: there is evil. Am I a figment of it? There is so much guilt in my heart that I feel as if I am a vile demon. So why did I continue with this charade? I am not sure. If I am still alive, then I am wrestling with that question. What provoked the events that occurred that day? And worse yet, that evening?

As I continued to rummage through a nearby garbage can, a man in an immaculate suit emerged from the building. Dr. Jack Worth made a beeline for the agent. They walked through the plaza together. Worth made erratic gestures. He was panicking. Of course, he would. A serial killer who was targeting him was still on the hunt.

I grabbed a half-eaten hamburger from the can and ate it on behalf of a curious passerby who shuddered as our eyes met.

The federal agent let his coat drift back a bit, which exposed the leather of a shoulder holster. The law was out in full force. They knew that I was around. Several cops in plainclothes tried to look inconspicuous. Gabriel Brimstone spent years picking a cop out in a crowd. He knew that if you have to *try* to look innocent, then you would stick out like a sore thumb.

I didn't dare get too close to them. I would have been pegged in a second. However, I did get information. Worth was afraid. He must know where Winthrop's wife and son were, and they were in federal custody. It wasn't encouraging news, but it was news nonetheless.

I made my way back into the parking ramp. Several of the federal surveillance agents moved about, searching for … well … me. I went through a couple of the garbage cans and even asked an agent for money for food. That day in the ramp, I made ten bucks and found out the guys were armed with Glocks.

I knew where the surveillance cameras were placed. It allowed me to stay beneath one of them in the shadows of a parked SUV. An agent passed by a moment after I untapped the pipe from my leg. My hand ached with the tension from gripping the pipe too tight. The agent scanned the darkness; his eyes squinted. His suspicion slapped me across the face. I knew the fed had a feeling that he was not alone.

My knuckles were white and my hand was trembling. I ached to kill him but had the humanity to try to fight the urge. The young federal agent drifted past me. I let out a sigh of relief from the darkness more from the fact that I didn't act than the idea that he nearly saw me. As I continued searching the ramp, I came across the car that I was searching for minutes before more feds began to mill about. My pulse raced while my hand continued to throb. I did not want more blood on my hands. *Why?* It wondered. *There is so much of it on your hands anyway. Will you even notice another pint? Or quart? Or … gallon?* Valimus/Gabriel Brimstone/Richard Stoker/The Tooth Fairy was right.

At this point in the narrative, I have to wonder: what you call me? Am I Valimus? Is that Demon in my head really my addiction? Am I *my* addiction? Am I defined by it? Every morning when I look at myself in the mirror and my tongue is thick with need, I make an effort to not drink. I "work the steps" as I should. Am I merely an addict? We talk about not being defined by our addiction but allowing it to shape the decisions that we make. It's about taking ownership for our actions, and not allowing out choices to propel us into a situation where we can use again. At that point, my addiction ruled me. I let it take over all of me. Was I my addiction during those hours/days?

Am I Gabriel Brimstone? Am I a fearless vampire hunter who is battling his inner demons and holding onto his humanity/sanity by not giving into his dark passions?

Could it be that I am this virtual unknown called Richard Stoker? Am I the vague memories of a man with a wife and son? Am I a troubled man who hears the shrieks of a woman who may be his wife, the tears of a child who may be his son, and the echoes of a shotgun blast in a cold, rainy night? Am I this man that I've been seeking since I stepped foot in Culver's Bay?

How do *you* see me? You, the passive observer who is reading the journals of a man who can never get to you. You, who reads this in the dead of night, will look out into the inky blackness of your window and not see me watching you. You think I am locked up. The virus has spread. It has already infected another. By reading my words, you have become a part of this. The power of knowledge is the simple fact that these words cannot be unread. Knowledge cannot be *un*learned. Knowledge demands action.

That is why it is so dangerous.

With that, I urge you to continue reading, to explore this demon that is in my head and has now crept inside of *yours*...

I stayed in the shadows of the car that belonged to Dr. Jack Worth. Even though federal agents infested the ramp, I never moved. As the spider that crawls along your face while you sleep, I stayed motionless as they crawled along the dark structure. Much like the spider, the feds slowly moved away. The afternoon wore along as Worth worked in his office, unaware that Death was waiting.

As it does for us all.

Inevitably the doctor's footsteps echoed in the dim, concrete structure. I held my breath and licked my lips; the suspense tasted like warm honey fresh from a hive. The jingle of his keys hurt my ears. That single spike of anger pumped the blood into my limbs even faster. The closer he got, the more tangible my anticipation became.

He crossed over to the driver's side of the car. The poor bastard never saw me. The pipe connected with the base of his skull.

I must not have hit him hard enough.

"Wha-what's going on?" His voice was shaky. I knew he had a concussion. His slurred speech and rolling eye movements as he lay trussed up along the backseat of the sedan told me that.

Something told me it would be a long night.

"I figured it all out." My voice was gravelly. It got that way whenever I was pissed off or tired.

I was both.

This wasn't adding up to anything good for Dr. Worth.

"Gabe? Is that you?"

"No."

"It is you. What's going on? Why did–"

"No, it isn't. I told you I figured it all out." There was a pause. I watched as the sun continued its descent behind the skyscrapers. Shadows grew in strength and swallowed reality. "Tell me about Richard Stoker and why you insisted on following him."

Even in the rearview mirror I could see the spineless maggot squirm.

"Tell me about him!" The car swerved. Taking careful, deep breaths, I steadied myself.

"How did you know–"

"Rachel told me..." Our eyes met in the rearview mirror, "...before I killed her."

"Dear God," he whispered. "Why?"

"She's an Indigo Child." I spat every word. "An abomination that will spell the end of the world. Just like … just like…" It was on the tip of my tongue. Why couldn't I recall it? What was I trying to recall?

"Like Eric?"

"Eric?" I remembered Alfonso's story. He whispered it to me just before I killed him. Right?

"Stoker's son. *Your* son." Then I remembered it. I mean *really* remembered it. Both realities began to converge. Alfonso wasn't doing the talking that night in the sewers. It was … *me*. I told *him* about my family. I told him how I was seeing psychic patterns in my son. I saw him developing abilities that were eerie and … familiar. The world became blurry and wet. I shook my head as the thunderclap explosion echoed in my mind again. It was the explosion of thunder.

The steps were long. It seemed like it took forever to get to the top of them. The barrel of the 12-gauge shotgun carved a trench in the thick carpet as I made my way to the room. The door was closed, but I knew what would be on the other side of it.

"Is that you, Daddy?" a small voice called from inside.

"Yes, son," I choked as I loaded a shell into the weapon. "I'm coming in…"

"No!"

"I'm sorry, Richard. I am so sorry, but this … this is *not* going to bring your family back!"

"Where are they?" I turned onto an on ramp that led to the outskirts of Culver's Bay.

"Their graves are-"

"No! Not … them." I took a deep breath. "The Winthrops."

"Dear God, no!"

"God has nothing to do with this." I smiled as I let Valimus in. "Try the other guy." The city faded away as I took Dr. Worth to a place where no one would hear his screams.

Worth screamed in the car until he passed out from exhaustion. When he came to, he found himself bound by his wrists in the basement of an abandoned factory in by the docks. Yeah, there was no one for miles, and if anyone was around, they wouldn't be speaking. At least, they wouldn't when they heard the screams.

I remember those screams well. It's something I will never forget, much like the woman's screams that haunt my dreams.

He came to and stared at the thick length of chain that held him fast to his position in the middle of the main floor.

"G-G-Gabe...?"

I smiled, looking up from my copy of the Alcoholics Anonymous book. "'Made direct amends to such people wherever possible, except when to do so would injure them or others,'" I read. My voice echoed along the high walls. A rat scurried off into the darkness. My mouth watered at the thought of drinking its blood. If it was true that I wasn't a vampire, then what fueled my lust for draining its small body of its life force? Worse yet, what made me want to do that to the good doctor? "We all have to make amends to someone. We all have screwed someone over in our pasts. It's part of human nature, don't you think? It's what makes us ... human." I looked up from the book, a dark smile on my face. "You think I'm human, don't you?" I dropped the AA book onto the floor.

"Of course, I do!" Worth stated, albeit a bit too fast for my liking. "You are a man! You don't need to-"

"To do what?" I interrupted. "To listen to myself? Is that what I shouldn't do? If I don't listen to myself, then who do I listen to? Who do I trust?"

"Me!" Desperation made his body reek, causing me to laugh.

"You are very funny. That sense of humor will serve you very well." I paced in front of him.

"You don't know what you're doing. I can save you. The police ... they want to execute you for what you've done."

I nodded. "I know. They don't believe that what I'm doing needs to be done for the better of mankind." Looking into his eyes, I saw his mind calculating. It caused my grin to widen. "Does it matter? It would be the answer for Valimus and Brimstone. Valimus thinks that to progress human evolution, the Turning of humans into vampires in the next step. Brimstone believes that he is the last bastion of hope for the human race to survive this potential pandemic."

"Y-you're a ... a ... g-"

"Good?" Moving with the speed of a viper, I stood mere millimeters in front of him. The sweat of his fear was an intoxicating aroma. "Is that what you were going to say? Does a 'good' man chain a man from the ceiling with every intention to torture him to death and drink the marrow from his bones if he doesn't tell him what he wants to know?" I eyed the heavy Bowie knife in my hand, turning the blade over in my hands. I became hypnotized by the rhythm of the dim lights reflecting off the steel. "I know Winthrop wanted you to keep an eye on me and you did so out of guilt. You were having an affair with his wife and felt even guiltier when he went missing because you knew deep down that he was dead. You knew and you still screwed his wife." I placed the cold steel against Worth's left cheek, and then locked our gazes together. Once he noticed the insanity that filled my gaze, the delicious panic set in. "This whole addiction and recovery thing is a lot harder than I thought. I never thought this would be a walk in the park, but I had no idea it would be this difficult. Those twelve steps are kicking my ass!" I laughed. "It takes dedication, focus, and a single-minded commitment. All of which were traits I thought I had." I used the blade's edge to shave some stubble from his face. The cowardly doctor whimpered and his bladder released. The stench filled my nostrils, and I laughed again. I looked down and saw the puddle at his feet. "Yeah, I'd be scared, too."

"Please, G-G-"

"What name *would* you call me? I've been searching for the right answer to that. Am I Richard Stoker? You insist on calling me Gabriel Brimstone, but that seems to be a name that I made up, or at least got from a crappy paperback novel, but is that really who I see myself as? The media have labeled me The Tooth Fairy." I dropped the knife onto the floor with a loud clatter; it skidded to a stop next to the AA book that fell onto the page describing the ninth step. Slowly, almost theatrically, I reached into my jacket pocket and pulled out a pair of rusty pliers. The grin faded onto my face and I used my empty hand to force his mouth open. He screamed as the rough steel grated across his white teeth. "Let's just go with that, shall we?"

After I stopped removing teeth, I began slicing with the knife. His screams acted as a score to my bloody work. The warm, salty fluid that drained down my eyes was not the blood of my victim, it was tears. I knew there was no coming back from this. Not this. It was true that Dr. Worth was an opportunistic creature who used the death of a colleague to seduce his lonely wife, but did he deserve to die like he did? Believe it or not, the worst thing wasn't the murder of this leech. The worst part of this whole sordid tableau was the fact that I enjoyed what I did to him. I enjoyed making him scream and making him suffer before he gave that last sigh of relief, letting me know that death had already claimed him.

The time for making amends has passed, I thought as I picked up the bloody book and stared at the ninth step. There was no way I would be able to come back from all of this. I couldn't continue living in a delusion, but I could not help but continue to play the part of the hero. Something compelled me to continue with this absurd, macabre farce.

Know thyself, my mind whispered to me. *Know thyself.*

Step Ten

"Continued to take personal inventory and, when we were wrong, promptly admitted it."

It took two teeth to get Worth to tell me Jessica and Ryan Winthrop's whereabouts. *Not bad*, I thought. Unfortunately for him, I continued to take ten other teeth from his face.

That wasn't the worst of it. I'll let you think of what that could be.

Worth's cries and pleas for mercy fell on deaf ears. As Gabriel Brimstone, I was an unforgiving bastard, but I was nowhere near as cruel or demented as I was that night. I did so much to him that late afternoon. It went well into the night, and neither of us stopped until we were tired. I thought Dr. Jack Worth was dead, but he wasn't. It wasn't until day seven of my trial that I found out that he was still alive. For a long time, I thought I had taken his life, but in actuality, all I took was his mind ... and soul.

Dr. Worth never testified at my trial. I heard rumors that he screams every time the sun sets and he looks out the window of his sanitarium waiting for me to take him. Sometimes I smile at that thought. Since that day where I took his mind and left him with fears of monsters that lurked in the dark, I had become a monster. I did not care about anything that happened to me or my mind.

Which didn't bode well for the Winthrop survivors.

By the time I was able to wash Worth's blood from my hands and face, clean the bloody knife and pliers, and angle Worth's car north, my mind had started to slow down. An eerie calm choked the stress out of me. My innards were cold – the preternatural cold that I had convinced myself came from the depths of hell. The expressway pushed away the city, giving way to rural landscapes, tall trees, and fewer buildings. A haze lifted from my mind. I saw myself for what I was.

Richard Stoker: psychotic.

It was strangely liberating.

I recalled that stormy night over five years ago. The world exploded in a white flash of lightning and a deluge of water. "Moment of clarity" is what they refer to it in my meetings.

I had climbed up the stairs; the shotgun was heavy in my cradled grip. My heart thudded, nearly cracking a rib. Tears streamed down my face, wetting the carpet. *He is sick.* That was the first time the Voices appeared. They spoke so softly that I strained to hear them again.

I approached my son's door. While I paused, his faint voice was muffled by the woods, but I could still hear him talking.

"Things are going to be different. You'll see. My dad will hug me and take me to games and we'll go fishing and-" His words were too low to be heard. "My dad loves me."

The shotgun shivered in my hand. *They* were getting to him.

Just as they did me!

I opened the door and felt the dam behind my eyes give way when I saw the whites of my son's eyes. "I do love him," I whispered so he could barely hear me.

I pulled the trigger.

The reverie nearly drove me into a guardrail. The blaring horns of passersby startled me into reality … *this* reality. I swerved to regain control over Worth's luxury sedan. Before I knew it, healthy trees, verdant fields and the sounds of chirping birds peppered the landscape. The edges of the sun brushed the horizon. The orb was a fierce red, the red of blood and murderous intentions. The cabin was minutes away, according to the blood-speckled paper that Worth used to write the location. After that, I worked him over for three hours and left him in a pool of his own blood. Of course, I was wrong about the portly doctor. I see that now. He wasn't a weakling. I would have thought that anyone would have died from the torture that I had inflicted on him. A weakling could not have survived that kind of punishment.

Taking the next off ramp, I made a hard right and took a dirt road that consumed the world around me. The world became organic. Everything around me was alive. The thick branches of the oaks surrounding me eclipsed the sun. The world grew darker.

I was home.

I felt a kinship with the world around me. It was alive and every little inch of my surroundings hummed with a heartbeat that was individualized, much like the psyches that lived inside of my mind: Gabriel Brimstone, Valimus, Richard Stoker, and the creature I was at that very moment. At that moment, I knew that reality was individual perceptions drawn with a broad brush that we all agree to. Each of us has a different, individual reality, but there are millions of little parallels that each perception has in common. These commonalities are "reality." Brimstone and Valimus operated under a different code of ethics within their realities. Their realities converged only because the laws that governed them were the same. My reality is different from yours. Fortunately for you, my reality is confined into a small environment and it will never intersect with yours...

Pray that it never does.

My reality converged violently with the Winthrops' that cool Friday night. Forensic scientists and biographers all relay it differently, but only I can give you the real scoop. Do you want to know what happened? Remember, once you learn it, you cannot *un*learn it.

****

The cabin was lit, but the curtains in the window were drawn. I kept the front end of the sedan away from the structure. The last thing I wanted was for the headlights to warn them of my arrival.

I parked about a hundred yards away from the cabin and stepped into the cool, living darkness. The Bowie knife was no longer slick with blood … yet.

The doctors tell me that what I was feeling that night was an adrenaline rush. They say that every time I would describe my heightened sensory awareness, the unusual coldness that would overwhelm my skin, making me feel as if I was in a meat locker. Even now I have my doubts. The peaceful feeling that dripped from my pores is just a "byproduct of my sociopathic tendencies."

I could feel Ryan in the cabin. He, like Rachel, was an Indigo Child. There are those who are touched with a power that was beyond the limits of humanity. Whether you believe my world to be delusional or not, this is based on fact. My son was an indigo, just like me.

Those dreams that came true, the Voices in my head … the Demon … is proof of that. Rachel succumbed to alcohol and drugs to quiet those dreams. My son would talk to spirits. Ryan Winthrop, the son of Malf … I mean … David Winthrop … was an indigo. He told me this in our therapy sessions at the Facility what I later learned was Amhearst. Isn't it funny? I returned home to finish what I started, but I was unaware of that. I learned that the house Jessica Winthrop was at reminded me of my own. That explained the déjà vu that I felt all those months ago. I committed the same action I did on my family on my therapist's family, but then I was unsuccessful. Dr. Winthrop told me about his childhood abilities of predicting the future. He told me a few things about himself that I shouldn't have learned. It was why I buried him in a lonely stretch of sand several miles out-side of Vegas.

Dr. Winthrop was a good man; upon retrospection, I see that now. His arrogance allowed certain pieces of himself to slip from his loose lips. Pride comes before a fall.

Please forgive me if I seem to be procrastinating from tell-ing the end of this sordid tale. Maybe I am doing this to savor the moments, much like of my victims. Sometimes the memories come back to me and others … well, they are hazy at times. I still find it difficult to recall the incidents that followed, not only be-cause of the medication I am on, but also because this reminds me that the whole sordid incident is still unresolved. What you read in the newspapers … the murders, the gruesome remains … they are still being committed. The most horrifying part of this story is that once you put this book down, you will go out at night and the monster … the *other* monster … is still out there. Yes, the monster at the end of this book is the narrator; however, this narrator, as unreliable as he may be, is not the only monster. As you read this, something out there, the monster, the creature, the demon, may be looking at *you*.

Yet, I digress…

The remainder of the story comes to me in my dreams. I do recall the soft earth beneath my feet, the firm grip on the ser-rated knife, the "adrenaline rush." All of it is a memory induced by a medicated slumber.

The planks that made up the porch creaked as I stepped onto them. The soft laughter that I heard within stilled. I know evil lay within that shack. I ran my hands along the solid wood of the cabin and pressed my ear against the cool surface. It hummed with life … a life that my fragile psyche demanded to end. The hard steel slid against the wood, scraping against the surface. My heart beat at a triple time cadence. I crept to a nearby window and stared through a crack made in the curtains that weren't closed. I watched as Jessica Winthrop smiled at her son over a board game. They both looked down at the board while little Ryan rolled the dice. He moved a game piece three spaces and laughed. You wouldn't have known that only a week or so before, they were being stalked by a monster.

The cabin belonged to Jack. He and his wife used to go there each summer. He would write his professional essays and books. She would go there to escape the hustle and bustle of city life. There was a pond several yards away. He would go there with her and they would fish. That was when they were happy. Now, he used it when his wife would call him for alimony. She knew he used it to get away from reality but did press the issue. He screamed all of this to me and more before he passed out due to blood loss and exhaustion.

I knew that Jack, Jessica, and Ryan went to the cabin many times. Jack and Ryan would go down to the pond to fish. Ryan even caught a walleye there once. It is one of his fondest memories. Little did Ryan know that it was Jack's fondest memory as well. You see, Jack never had kids. He had a low sperm count. I watched Ryan smile as he moved his board piece across the game board. He laughed with his mother and for a moment I remembered playing a game with my son … I mean, Richard's son.

"Monopoly," I whispered the game we used to play. "Eric liked the race car." I twirled the knife in my hand. I took a deep breath and looked at the crisp night sky. The world went quiet, as if the creatures of the forest knew what was about to happen and were holding their breath in grim anticipation.

I circled the house to the large electric cable that led from the house to a shed nearby with a generator. Something made me pause as I took the cable into my hands. The endgame would begin once that cord was severed. They would know that the demon was stalking them again. They would know that their luck had finally run out.

Was I ready for this? Once it was over, finally over, what then? What was the next thing to do once the Winthrops were dead? The "prophecy" would be done. I would have "saved the world." What happens next? Would the credits roll and the lights would fade to black? Would my reality end? The world would continue unabated. The hero will have saved mankind and allowed man to continue with his killing, lying, and cheating. What does a hero do after he has saved the world? If this was a movie, he would wait until the sequel.

He would do it all over again.

How long would this go on? Let's say I find another delusional war. Let's even say I decide to forget the past month and I find another prophecy and I find another reason to start this whole thing over again. What happens after that? Do I continue to do this again and again until someone like Agent Andrews succeeds in killing me?

"I guess there's only one way to find out." I smiled as I sawed through the cord and severing the connection to the generator. The whole cabin went dark.

Their screams came soon after that.

****

I closed my eyes and imagined the two of them running through the cabin, screaming.

"Mom! Mom! It's the monster. I know it. It's the monster." The kid was right.

I experienced déjà vu again as I jogged over to their blue Hyundai and punctured the tires with my blade. Returning to the cabin, I crouched/walked to the rear of the structure and peered in through a window. The bedroom was spartanly furnished. A bed and dresser were the only furniture in the room. On the opposite side of the window was a closet that was cracked. I knew they weren't hiding in there. Ryan would never feel the same way about closets again, I bet. Foraging around on the soft earth, I found two rocks about the size of my fist and lobbed one through the bedroom window. Their screams filled the forest; they were no longer muffled by the glass and wood of the cabin. Then, I jogged to the front of the house and tossed the other rock through the front window. The picture pane exploded into razor shards that rained inside the structure. I hesitated. Should I step through the threshold and become that monster I dreaded, the demon that I began fighting?

Do it, the monster in me advised.

"No," I whispered. "I ... I ... I can't do it."

My brain exploded. The world brightened; reality glowed in front of me.

That is the last thing I remembered, but that is not the end.

Not for me.

****

I knew that Gabriel Brimstone was weak, and that I had to take over. He was having an identity crisis as his world had imploded in on himself due to the fact that he was a brilliant detective. I had warned him, even fogged his perception of reality as I did with the whole "prophecy" red herring from the truth. Sometimes it is better to not know the truth. He learned the hard way that life is hard. His is a fragile mind. All I was doing was trying to protect his psyche. I wanted to spare Richard/Gabriel the guilt of his murderous tendencies.

So I became Valimus. It is what he needed. He needed someone to blame. Yet, I knew that his lack of knowledge would be his undoing, as is his curious nature.

Call me what you may: conscience, Demon as he did, or Savior as he does. That is unimportant. Are we a monster because we are trying to protect our identity? This is survival.

It is in this spirit that I took the knife in an upside-down grip and entered the cabin, fully committed to commit a most heinous action.

Throughout this whole journal, written in flesh and blood, Gabriel/Richard has referred to me as "Valimus," so perhaps that is the best way to refer to myself here. I am writing this because the "hero" will have no recollection of the events he wishes to remember. He will also have no recollection of the text that I am penning right at this moment. As such, those of you reading must know that he was unconscious during those moments.

Save for a few steps upon broken glass, I moved within the cab-in soundlessly. My breathing was controlled, shallow, like a predator. And like a predator, I relied on my other senses to zero in on my prey. Jessica wore the same perfume from the night that Gabriel stalked her, the night he let her go. What a disappointment he was that evening.

I checked the living room where they played their game. It was empty. I moved to the kitchen and noticed that a large butcher knife was missing from a cutlery board. It was hard not to smile and praise my victim. Bravo! I thought.

I studied my surroundings, knowing they would leave a sign of their location. Gabriel Brimstone was a hunter; he could be quite calcu-lating when need be. I left many clues in his wake for him to eliminate people that he would think of as preternaturals, superhumans, and vampires ... mythical creatures that would tap into the self-loathing that he had due to abilities he saw in himself and in his son. In short, I used that self-loathing to create a world that he would be able to estab-lish some importance within. However, I did not see him as being smart enough to break through that reality. I was right for the most part. He didn't break it; he blurred the lines. His "hunter" skills were compro-mised. As such, I could not trust him to clean up this mess.

This whole thing was a mess. I knew we were both at fault. Our weaknesses and fragile psyche turned a weakened father into a beast. Our addiction was not to blood, but to fantasy, to thinking we were something that we weren't. Richard should have known that he was not cut out to be a family man. He should have known that we weren't well. Now, I was created to clean up a mess that I helped to create. I tried to have him do it himself, but the old saying proved true:

If you want something done right, you have to do it yourself.

I sighed and scanned the room. Upon closer inspection, I found a scrap of Jessica's flannel shirt torn and hanging from a bent nail in the doorway that led to a long hall. There was another bed-room that led off into that direction. I smelled the air and could pick up the faintest hint of sweat.

The smell of fear.

The door to the room was shut. It was the only room left. However, I knew there was a window in that room. I turned away *and retreated back to the entrance to the cabin. I was just in time to see them running towards the pond.*

I do hate it when they run.

Step Eleven

"Sought through prayer and meditation to improve our conscious contact with God, as we understood Him, praying only for knowledge of His will for us and the power to carry that out."

The wind had whipped up in frenzy, as if it went along with my mood. The moon was large, silver and bright. It was the perfect light for stalking prey. I felt an exhilaration fill me like a pitcher of water. Part of me wanted to howl, scream my excitement and joy. I followed the broken branches and slight footprints. Jessica was leading her son towards the pond. Perhaps there was a boat there that could take them across the water. I knew I wasn't far behind. I heard the woman swear as she saw the ruined tires of her potential getaway car.

I wasn't too far behind them. Sometimes I heard their footfalls on the soft, wet grass. The ground gave way the closer we got to the pond. The branches of the nearby trees snapped at me. A few twigs left lashed cuts across my face, but I didn't care. When the forest gave way to the pond, there was nothing to greet me but the silence.

The deafening silence.

I found them in the water. Ryan was near the stalks of weeds that grew from the black surface. Jessica, with dark strands of hair framing her face, slashed at me with her fingernails. She hissed at me while her son cried in the background.

"I won't let you take my son!" she screamed.

Her insanity gave her strength. I was strangely detached from the situation. Her claws raked the air around me. I dodged and weaved as she led me out into the waters. I felt like Gabriel was watching from

154

afar and I knew he was thinking of Susan, his wife. Yes, Gabriel, Susan would have had the same look on her face had she known what you did to her son.

A wild slash by the woman knocked the Bowie knife from my grasp. It sank beneath the waters. Soon after, anger swelled inside of me like an oncoming wave. Before I knew what was happening, I grabbed her by the throat. Her eyes widened, knowing the inevitable was coming. She scratched my arms, wrists, and face. Her mouth dropped open and went slack. She was trying to say something. Was she begging? No. She wasn't the type. Was she going to curse me with her last breath? No.

I slackened my grip, to see what she would say. Her eyes locked onto mine. Her hands gripped my jacket, then her wide orbs rolled to her right; to the shore.

To her son.

"Run." That was the last thing she would ever say.

Her body went slack, heavy in my hands.

I looked towards the shoreline in time to see a little black shadow detach itself from the reeds and run in the opposite direction. Jessica Winthrop's corpse sank beneath the dark waves. She disappeared by the time I got ashore.

This was not going according to plan. I had no intentions of killing them slowly, and I had strangled Jessica and had no weapon to kill the child. I never wanted to kill a kid with my bare hands. I realized I was headed back to the cabin. The kid would be able to find a nice hiding place inside with the head start that I gave him.

Moments later, I stood in the doorway of the cabin. My shadow cast a long deep shadow into the rustic abode. I was tired of doing this; I wanted it to be over.

"Ryan, please come out. You do not know just how tired I am of this." I crossed the threshold and sighed. "Please. I want it to be over like you do." It took me a few minutes to search the living room. What does a monster do to lure its victim into the open? I could feel Gabriel coming back… "You can see me for what I am, can't you?" I paused, trying to push him back. "Even though I walk on two legs, have two hands, two feet, a torso and a head … but you don't see me as human, do you?" I checked the other room, the one I hadn't checked earlier. "I'm

sure you know that was me in your closet." I headed for a closet that was nearby. "Listen, kid. I'm not really a monster. I don't want to kill you. I have hurt a lot of people and I don't want to do it anymore." It was the truth. "If you come out, I promise I won't harm a hair on your head." Now, that was a lie. My hand closed over the doorknob to the closet. I could practically taste my prey. On the count of three, I flung open the door.

Much to my chagrin, I was met by nothing.

But I did hear Ryan's feet pounding the earth. He rushed right past me, moving from underneath the bed. With a roar, I swung the blade in a vicious arc. He screamed as the blade cleaved into his arm. An angry crimson smear darkened the wall. I roared again and charged after him. I was mere inches away from him; he screamed and burst through the front door. I swore under my breath and through the threshold into the forested darkness...

And into the crosshairs of the familiar FBI agent waiting to take me in.

"Gabriel Brimstone, aka Richard Stoker, you are under arrest. Place your hands in the air."

I couldn't be taken in, I thought. I have to see this through to the end.

So I charged the cop.

And he fired.

I heard the roar of his automatic and all I remember after that is this Facility.

****

Five months later: The infirmary at the institute was top notch, so after a few months of rehab, I was in a cell of my own. To be honest, I don't remember what happened after I arrived at the cabin. The doctors told me I was lucky. For five minutes, my heart stopped. Clinically, I was dead. So it stood to reason I did not remember the events that occurred on that October night. I have read the previous entry and noticed someone had filled in the blanks. My court appointed attorney told me a handwriting sample was taken and the previous entry was written by me! How was this possible? I didn't know the whole story. I pieced it all together from what brief flashes of memory have come back to me.

I don't recall Agent Andrews holding the Beretta, my Beretta, in his hands telling me to get on the ground or he would blow my head off.

I do recall sitting in a police station watching a video that a passerby took with their cell phone of me inside a motel room dancing while I chewed at a woman's heart, a woman who I once thought of as Miranda Baltimore. "Revel in the massacre! Drink! Drink! Drink!" I remember Valimus saying that in my mind, but I don't remember saying it. I am sure all the other videos they showed at the trial are uploaded on YouTube or something.

The rest of it you can read in the bestsellers and online: the audio of my confession, the televised court proceedings, the non-fiction books and I guess they're making a movie. As long as one of those damned *Twilight* kids don't have a role in it, I'll be just fine.

I'm sure Andrews will be a bona fide celebrity. He told me that the reason he had such an itch to scratch. The owner of the Beretta I used was his brother, a Philadelphia cop.

Small world, I guess.

He visited me a few times to interview me. I would have thought that since he had family that was a victim of my war, he would have been too close to the case.

"You say you don't remember what happened the night you killed Jessica Winthrop and maimed Dr. Jack Worth, but you've written about it in your journal. How do you explain that?" the federal agent asked one afternoon.

"I can't. I don't remember writing it. It sounds like something Valimus would have written, but-"

"But you know that it's not real."

We sat across from each other in metal chairs. A matching table sat between us. He wore another crisp suit and I still wore my white jumpsuit. I was chained to the table. A pair of cuffs held me close to the flat surface. I nodded. "I do remember doing what I did to Dr. Worth. I don't remember anything after arriving at the cabin that night." We'd gone over this at least ten times. "How is he? The doctor, I mean."

Andrews shook his head. "He's still under the impression that you actually are a vampire. The forensic crew knows you ingested some of his flesh and blood. You stripped him of twenty percent of his skin and you removed several of his teeth." He leaned across the table and asked. "The teeth ... why?"

"It strips the vampire of its power."

"We retrieved the sack from your motel room." He took a deep breath, as if the very memory of what I did in that room caused him to become nauseous. "You didn't think of him as a vampire. Why the teeth?"

"When two realities start converging, it creates confusion. I knew he wasn't a vampire but ... but..." I shook my head. "I needed to be sure. He was helping Malfric and-"

"You mean Dr. Winthrop."

"Yes." It was my turn to look exasperated. "Look, Andrews. I apologized for what I did. I took ownership of my actions, those I remember and those I don't. The jury saw fit to keep me here for the rest of my life. It's over. What more do you want from me?"

"Two things: The first one is this." He opened up a briefcase that sat next to his chair and placed a folder on top of the table. He slid it across the table and I opened it. I saw black and white photographs of bodies with their throats torn out. Some had decapitated heads strewn across the floor. Blood covered the grimy walls of the background. "These photographs were taken within the past three weeks. Someone is using your MO." My body shook ever so slightly, but it was enough for the cop to notice. "You know something, don't you?" I couldn't keep the fear from my face.

"Dear, God," I prayed. "Please, no." Tears fell from my eyes.

"What is it?" His fist slammed against the table.

"I am trying to convince myself, but I was right. Dammit, I was right." My body shook as tears fell.

"Stoker, what the hell are you talking about?"

"You cannot stop it because you don't believe."

"Believe in what?"

"You just don't believe!" I rocked my body in the chair. The door opened and two orderlies came in. One of them, as usual, had a syringe. "I am truly damned! I died, don't you see? I have died and I came back, just like Valimus said … just like … I … am."

"He's done, Special Agent," one of the two orderlies said while he prepped my cocktail.

"No!"

I never saw the needle, but I felt it in my bicep. "God, grant me the serenity to accept the things that I cannot change, the courage to change the things that I can, and the wisdom to know the difference!" I yelled this at the top of my lungs. "God, please keep a watch over me. Don't let me Turn. Please, I beg of you. I know you are a benevolent God."

I remembered people like Caleb, Rachel, and all the people in my war that showed me kindness, those victims who showed me what vulnerability was, and those enemies who showed me what can happen when I showed strength and power. "You have showed me a family that loved me and I returned that love in the only way that I knew." That love was returned in violence, swift and sure. My life flashed before my eyes and I knew my cell would be my coffin.

The chemicals began to work, but I continued to rant and rave. "She's coming! She's coming for me! She will be riding a pale horse! She will be painting a canvas of flesh and blood, just as I did! Andrews, you have to stop her! Please … please…" The colors and lights blurred together into a violent tapestry of whites and reds.

Step Twelve

"Having had a spiritual awakening as the result of these Steps, we tried to carry this message to alcoholics, and to practice these principles in all our affairs."

Three months later:

So here I sit in this room that will not allow me to bash my head in, even if I was so inclined. I wear this nice cozy jacket with the long sleeves and I wait.

I wait for her.

In the meantime, I work my steps and I thank God for allowing me to get through each day. I read my AA book and my Bible, the second thing Andrews had for me. Apparently, a mysterious benefactor had given it to him to give to me. I will have to thank Caleb if ever he comes to visit me. I read my Bible and pray for forgiveness. Once I even met with a priest and asked for salvation. The man even says that God forgives me. I find that hard to believe.

I try to go through the steps again, maybe next time I will get it right. I still Thirst. Now, more than ever. Yet, I do know that "working the steps" and reading my Bible is futile. One day, she will come for me. She will take my life because she knows what I am and that I should not be. I am still hoping for that "spiritual awakening." Perhaps that will come in time. Can a damned soul receive a spiritual awakening? I am not sure, nor am I sure if that is what I want now.

My captors do not visit me often. Each time they have tried to visit me to exercise in the yard, or go to lunch, I will attack and try to drink their blood. Valimus was right all along. I did die, and I came back. At one time, I thought the world would be safe with me in this cell, but I know now this is far from the case. The agent and the media have labeled me as a lunatic. They say I am delusional and my reality of vampires is nothing short of imaginations and fantasies.

If that is so, then what about that rash of brutal vampire-like slayings of predators that plague this city? What about that woman who is preying on the denizens of Culver's Bay? What about that nice little girl we attacked in the sewers over a year ago?

The homeless denizens of what was once known as Dark City are being attacked and killed. I hear little urban legends that there is some demon who takes the form of an angel. They say that at night, if one goes outside at 2:15 a.m. and closes their eyes, while standing where Dark City used to be, and whisper her name, then she will appear. She will ask if the hapless person has spare change. Then, she will kill them and drain them of their blood. If Richard Stoker was neither Gabriel Brimstone nor Valimus, then would he have been able to infect that little homeless girl with a virus?

If you think so, then put this book down and go outside. Wait until it is pitch black outside and go out to take a deep breath of that cool darkness.

Close your eyes.

Do you believe enough to whisper her name? Do you believe in us enough to tempt fate, to risk your life? Go ahead. Do it. Whisper her name … Arlene.

I dare you.

About the Contributors

Gerald Browning:

Gerald has crafted his life around reading and writing. Ever since working on a book report at the age of seven, he has fallen in love with the written word. He received a Bachelor's of Arts in English at The University of Michigan – Flint and a Master's Degree in English Studies from Illinois State University. He is pursuing a Doctorate in Educational Leadership from Western Michigan University. He has written fiction for *Hardboiled Magazine, Necrotic Tissue, Detective Mystery Stories,* and, of course, *Night to Dawn,* where Gabriel Brimstone first graced the printed page. He also writes reviews for classic horror films *Bloody Disgusting,* a website devoted to horror films.

Gerald has taught English, Communications, Literature, and Speech at colleges such as The University of Michigan – Flint, Kettering University, and Baker College of Muskegon where he resides as Director of College Writing. He is a member of The Michigan Council of Teachers of English where he serves as Membership Chair.

As long as he continues to have nightmares, Gerald Browning will write. He is working on a follow up to *Demon in My Head* (working title: The Modern Prometheus).

He can be reached at geraldbrowning@hotmail.com.

**Teresa Jay**: Originating from the UK but now residing in the Canary Islands for the last 10 years, freelance artist Teresa Jay finds more time to devote to her love of art and painting. For more than 30 years she has been doodling with pencils and dabbling with watercolors. More recently she has been painting traditionally in oil and creating large canvases full of color and life. Sometimes she uses a more modern technique using software such as Photoshop, Corel Draw and Paint Shop Pro to produce her creations for online publications.

During her art career, she has produced countless illustrations, book covers and paintings. Along with published stories and poetry, she can be credited with award winning cover art and illustrations for author stories. Her work can be seen online and in print across the UK, US, Canada and Europe.

May 2011, she opened a new Exhibition in Puerto del Santiago (Tenerife, Spain) entitled Tutto per la vita (All for the life). She has over 30 works on show and is hoping to be selected to participate in the Capitals annual Art Festival. Should she win, there will be invitations to exhibit her work in a whirlwind trip across Spain and Italy.

Touching and spectacular "has been the inauguration; Tutto Per la vita" Some thirty of their works appeared, giving you a journey to Spain, Africa, America, Japan and Thailandia. The work was intense with feeling, in full color and textures, where figures, landscapes and moments will leave the visitor with a memory of a magical trip."

José Francisco Morales
Comisario de la Exposición (Tenerife)
http://www.artesigloxxi.org

I like to think that I am very versatile in my choice of subject matter - my new surroundings provide the inspiration for me to paint on a daily basis and the fact that others may enjoy

my work gives me the confidence to continue.
Website: http://teresatunaley.wixsite.com/artstopper

www.ingramcontent.com/pod-product-compliance
Lightning Source LLC
Chambersburg PA
CBHW052136170626
46812CB00004B/1450